THE

CHRISTMAS

LIST

Hillary Ibarra

This book is dedicated to several people:

First, to my husband Matthew, a very patient man who—even before we met in person—believed in me after reading an early version of this story. We have made a wonderful life together and he has never given up on me.

And to our four amazing children who helped me to rediscover this tale not long ago and make it better.

And to my father, Daniel Hylton, who has ever encouraged me.

This book is dedicated to my family with love and gratitude.

Contents

Snow

Every year at Christmastime the four Hoyle children prayed for presents and snow. The first came if the work was good for the father and mother, but the second was rarely fulfilled despite their earnest childish prayers. Snow seldom fell in Middle Tennessee in December.

But one year it did snow several days before Christmas.

Falling long from the gray-faced sky, it lined the windowsills of the Hoyle family home as they lay sleeping and shrouded the blackberry bushes and peach tree along the backyard fence. By the sloping driveway a massive walnut tree bore clouds of white, and a little dogwood standing alone in the front lawn cradled more in the curves of its slender branches.

A long dirt lane led up to the house, and beneath it a creek ran through a culvert. Into the cold, clear water of that stream the snow fell softly as if returning to an old friend.

Rising hazily above this resplendent garb of winter, the sun reflected brilliantly off the field of white behind the little blue house the Hoyles rented.

Jack, the father, was awake early that Sunday morning, analyzing the strange quality of the light that came through the windowpanes. He got up, pushing a mane of dark hair from his face, and looked outside.

His pale green eyes, the color of a frozen pond, surveyed more snow than he had seen since moving to the South with his young family. His stern and bearded face was softened by sleep and thoughts of a childhood in Idaho where winter always brought snow—something that was both a marvel and a headache.

The large, lazy flakes in Middle Tennessee usually evaporated as quickly and as silently as they fell, especially before January.

This time, however, those flakes had stayed, creating a cover of snow several inches deep.

He glanced at the bed where his wife stirred, rolling over to his side to place a hand where he had recently been. Her large brown eyes opened, and she turned her delicate face beneath her gently waving hair, fine as silk, to find him.

"Come here, honey," he said. "Come see this. You won't believe it."

She flipped back the covers and put on her robe and slippers.

"Did it snow?"

"Oh, yes," Jack said, and he smiled. "But not what they told us on the news last night. This is not 'occasional flurries'—it's deep and still snowing."

To the window she came, and he held back the curtains for her.

"It's beautiful," she said.

"It is," Jack agreed as Karen slipped an arm through his. He turned to look down at her and added, "But it won't help with work. It's going to hurt our Christmas."

As he spoke, they heard their four children waking up in the two bedrooms down the tiny hall.

The youngest of the Hoyle children, Nate and Heather, nicknamed Hoodoo, tripped over scattered Lincoln Logs and toy cars to look out the window.

"Hoodoo!" Nate looked from the frosted window to the wide brown eyes of his little sister. "You know what this means, don't you? No school tomorrow!"

Hoodoo jumped up and down. "Yes, yes, yes!"

Across the hall Vinca, the eldest, came out of her bedroom, and Annie covered her head with a pillow to ward off the shouts of her little sister. Vinca and Annie were close in age and had looked like twins in their tow-headed toddlerhood, but Vinca's hair had darkened to a soft brown. Annie alone was still fair-haired.

The kids came one by one into the bedroom of their parents with disheveled hair and rumpled pajamas, climbing over and pushing each other out of the way before jumping on their parents' bed. Their voices blended into a loud chatter of excitement.

"It snowed!" Vinca said, alerting them to this miracle.

We should go sledding," said Annie, flipping her straw-colored hair out of her face to reveal blue eyes alight with inspiration. "Down the big hill!"

"Yeah," added Nate, a reliable conspirator in such adventures. "But what can we use?"

"How about the cobbler pan?" said Karen. Her beautiful alabaster features were as youthful as a teenager's as she laughed at her own suggestion.

The enormous cobbler pan had been around forever, curved on the bottom but now misshapen from years of use. It fulfilled its destiny every summer when Karen made her deep-dish blackberry cobbler from the berries the family picked in late summer in the yard and fields near their home.

"It'll hold you, and it should go pretty fast despite the dents," she added, and the kids could hear her excitement for their upcoming adventure.

"There's Dad's old hubcaps, too," said Nate. "They're slick. Can we use them, Dad?"

"Sure, son. I don't need them. But right now, you kids have to clear out of the room so your mother and I can get dressed. Go on!"

Hoodoo, the only daughter to inherit both her momma's eye color and fine, dark hair, reached up her hand to rub her daddy's beard on the way out. Jack grimaced at the sharp tug on his chin, but he patted her back in a half-affectionate, half-irritated manner as she followed her siblings.

Annie, Nate and Hoodoo sat on the sagging brown couch looking out the big living room window with eager eyes, and a slender gray and white cat they called Sammy joined them there, rubbing against their shoulders affectionately and seeking warmth.

Vinca curled up in Jack's shaggy armchair with her black and white cat Tommy, Sammy's brother, and her bright blue eyes devoured the pages of a book as the fluffy tomcat attempted to loosen her snug embrace.

While Karen was making coffee, Jack leaned against the front door, feeling the chill seeping in as he gazed out the small rectangles of glass, thinking of bills and presents and wondering how on earth he could manage both.

When Karen placed a steaming cup of coffee in his hand, he said, "I'll have to get more wood."

"You better dress warm."

"Can we come, too?" Nate asked, and Jack nodded.

"Put warm clothes on!" Karen called after her scurrying children as they hurried to put on jeans and sweaters and mittens sent from their grandparents in Idaho. "Layer! It's wet out there."

Reuben, Jack's black Labrador dog, unusually large for his breed, lifted his big head from the concrete porch and turned his brown eyes to Jack, stiff and alert, when the family exited the house. The family's mutt Mandy was leaping across the snow's layers like a deer, her multi-colored coat accentuated by the landscape. She gave her funny half-howl when she saw Annie, her favorite person.

Jack picked up his ax, and then handed it into the mouth of his ever-loyal companion who was already trotting at his heels. They headed toward the field with the kids marching behind, making deep indentations in the snow.

The yard was enclosed by a barbed wire fence that separated it from the field the landlord rented to a local farmer who at various times pastured cows there, made hay, or grew corn. There was a wide gate in the fence, left open for many seasons when the cows had gone. Through it they went, past a drooping hedge of honeysuckle, burdened with snow and marooned in blossom-less sleep.

The fluffy and iridescent robe of snow that spread across the large field was full of possibilities. Annie dropped into its cold, wet embrace to carve out a snow angel, and then she took off running. Nate sped after, his thick brown hair ensnaring snowflakes, his instinct for mischief just as strong as hers.

"Daddy, is this the kind of snow that brought Frosty to life?" Hoodoo asked, slipping her mittened hand into her dad's bare, calloused one. "It's so sparkly. It's Christmas snow, right?"

Before Jack could answer his little girl, who had a sincere and longstanding love of snowmen, snowballs whizzed through the air, pitched in the direction of Jack, Hoodoo and Vinca. One splattered against the front of Vinca's jacket, and Nate and Annie's laughter echoed against the bare trees of the wood as they hurried to make more.

Hoodoo darted behind Jack, but Vinca rolled a perfect ball of snow and aimed at the nearest culprit, Annie, hitting her target squarely on the bottom as her back was turned.

Jack pulled Hoodoo out from behind him where she crouched, laughing nervously.

"C'mon," he said, stooping down and rolling a huge snowball. He threw it in the direction of Nate to ward off an attack, and then deftly rolled several more for ammunition before an idea struck him.

"Make forts!" Jack commanded with a grin.

His experience with such shelters became evident to his kids within minutes as his fort rose quickly and evenly.

Nate and Annie argued loudly about proper technique, shoving each other out of the way before finally splitting up to construct their own. Hoodoo slapped handfuls of snow into small and wobbly snowballs that she propped against Jack's fort as she glanced toward Nate. As his honorary little brother, she knew all too well how brutal his tactics could be. Vinca became engrossed in the art of erecting an elegant defensive structure that was doomed never to be finished before the first volley of enemy fire.

This time Jack was the first to get a shot off at Annie who had just lifted her fair head above her fort to search out a victim. The dogs barked and dodged back and forth as they were sprayed with the icy results of multiple impacts. Mandy tried to catch the snowballs with her mouth, jumping and colliding with human friends and decimating their forts. Reuben learned it was futile and sat near Jack, only rising to all fours and barking a warning when his master got hit. Jack's and the kids' faces grew ruddier with exertion and cold as they ducked, ran, and pitched. When one of Annie's snowballs struck

Vinca hard on the cheek, leaving an angry mark, Vinca glared at her younger sister and sometime rival and then stalked off toward the woods, only pausing to kick her sister's already ruined fort on the way.

"Okay, we're done!" said Jack, brushing off the last bits of ice melting on his thin coat. "Time to collect some wood."

Nate lobbed one last snowball at Hoodoo who had dodged behind their dad at every opportunity. It sprayed one of her small ears, so disproportionate to her already prominent nose.

"Hey!" said Hoodoo. "Daddy said stop!"

Nate grinned and took off running.

They entered the woods by a well-worn path they took often in the spring to a clearing where they held wiener roasts in the summertime. The woods were quiet with an intense silence that ever accompanies heavy snowfall. Despite the quiet, the snow accumulating upon the ground conveyed activity. On the strange, new carpet spread across the forest floor, the prints of little animals could be seen.

"It's so pretty out here, Daddy," Vinca said in a whisper.

"Why are you whispering?" asked Hoodoo in her—as usual—too loud voice.

"Because you'll scare all the animals away," answered Nate, and he quickly scaled a tree to see if she had done so.

"Watch this," said Annie to Vinca, and she performed a graceful ballerina leap off a blanketed tree stump, her long, gangly legs spreading wide for the maneuver.

Jack retrieved his ax from Reuben's maw and found a fallen branch to chop, secretly cursing the moisture in it. Nate came up to watch, every man's activity being fascinating to a growing boy.

"Can I use the ax, Dad?" Nate asked solemnly, his hands thrust deep into the pockets of his jacket with his black eyes earnestly trained on his father.

"No, son. It's pretty heavy. I don't want you to hurt yourself."

Nate stayed, watching his dad swing the ax with quick, precise motions.

"I wouldn't hurt myself, Dad," he said.

Jack paused and wiped little beads of sweat from his brow, "If you want to learn, son, I can teach you back at the house. Right now, I just need to get some wood."

Disappointed, Nate wandered off to terrorize his sisters.

They forgot animals as Annie, Nate and Hoodoo chased each other around trees and over stumps to wrestle each other down into the snow, and then they created more snow angels in the path, scraping against and revealing the earthy debris of autumn underneath. Nate again climbed a tree to look for turkeys and foxes.

"Come get some wood!" Jack called, and the three youngest raced and jostled each other while Vinca, prim and stoic, came behind.

Each of the younger three took up much more than they could carry and began staggering awkwardly back across the field toward the house, but Vinca carried hers in an orderly stack.

As Jack hauled a long tree branch over his shoulder across the field, Nate and Hoodoo ducked back and forth underneath it, wood sliding out from their arms.

"You two get up ahead of me and stay ahead of me," ordered Jack.

At the porch, they set down their wood by the small pile already there. Then they noisily stamped their feet all over the concrete porch to dislodge the snow before ushering into the house where they could smell breakfast cooking. The dogs pushed through behind, not caring one bit as they shook the moisture out of their coats by the woodstove.

Quickly peeling off their wet outer clothes by the door, the kids went to stand by the woodstove, too, wiggling their frozen fingers above its surface and hoping their momma would bring them hot cocoa for their chilled bodies.

The wood-burning stove, square and black, stood near the back wall in the middle of the long living room. Jack thrust two older, drier pieces of wood onto the glowing but irresolute bed of coals in its belly. He then blew on it for several minutes, withdrawing after each exhalation, until the coals bore flames that flickered between the pieces of wood and gnawed at them hungrily.

Karen set his breakfast of pancakes and hash browns on the grate of the stove and embraced her husband.

"You're cold," she said. "Let me get you some coffee."

The younger kids followed their mother into the narrow L-shaped kitchen, searching for their breakfast. After Hoodoo bumped into her mom and made her spill the coffee, Karen admonished, "Nate, Heather, you get out of here! I'll get your breakfast after I take care of your dad."

Hoodoo stuffed a spoonful of batter into her mouth before Annie slapped her hand away. Then Annie, who usually helped her mother, promised to make special banana pancakes for her little sister in an attempt to buy patience.

As the family sat around the wobbly fold-out table just outside the kitchen, the snow began to sputter again outside. It drifted with the sighing wind, twirled and caressed the window as the Hoyle kids watched, fascinated. Jack's skill with the stove had finally warmed their numb fingers and toes, and each began to envision an adventure on the big hill.

The children gathered in the kitchen with their breakfast dishes and looked out the back window at the far end of the field where the frosted hill sloped down between broad flanks covered by woodland. It was an impressive sight, glistening in the subdued mid-morning light.

"Are you guys ready to go sledding?" Annie asked.

"Let's get dressed," said Vinca. Though she rarely felt enticed by the hikes and explorations the other kids enjoyed among Tennessee's fields and forests, there was excitement in her voice. Being the oldest, she remembered the various homes her family had known before moving to Tennessee. They had traveled across the western United States where snow was plentiful.

The clothes from the morning jaunt were still uncomfortably wet, so they sought more jeans, socks, and sweaters, this time begging their dad for some of his thick socks to use as mittens.

"Mom, where's the cobbler pan?" Annie called as she bundled up.

"I'll get it." Karen rummaged through the kitchen cabinets and coaxed the beaten, much used pan from a dark cupboard corner and handed it to Vinca.

"Don't forget the hubcaps," Jack reminded Nate as he opened the front door for them.

With Vinca gripping the cobbler pan and Nate swinging a hubcap, they followed the path to the side of the house and slipped through the opening in the fence. They passed their ramshackle clubhouse, which had been a chicken coup when the landlord had lived on the property. It stood in a shallow hollow that split the enormous field into two sections, the smaller one on their left rarely explored. To the right the great hill rose before them, many yards away across the cornfield.

When they reached the hill at last, already wet and breathing hard, they halted to catch their breath as they stared up along its tall and inviting mass. Then they clambered to the top, cheering and panting.

Vinca and Annie attempted to sled in the hubcap and pan, but the snow wasn't as slick as it had looked from the house. It was a disjointed and discouraging trip to the bottom as their makeshift sleds stuck and slid, stuck, and slid again. The girls fought the hill for the ride they had craved.

When they returned to the top, Nate stated pragmatically, "We need to make paths. We have to pack the snow down."

Thus began the hard work before the fun, scooting on their bottoms and feet down a hill with rocks and frozen corn stalks buried beneath the snow. They used their hands to scratch out the detritus of other seasons. Despite their layered socks, their hands and feet grew cold and numb once more, and they rested periodically to rub the warmth back into them.

At the house Jack and Karen sat drinking more coffee and finishing their breakfast in newly acquired peace. Jack gazed out the window. His expression did not reflect awe and wonder, but consternation.

"I can't believe it's snowing again," he said in a tone to match his expression.

Karen glanced out and then silently watched her husband's features for several moments before saying, "The kids love it, though. It's a real treat for them."

"A real treat that will ruin their Christmas," said Jack. "We're short on the rent. We're low on groceries. We need to work. How much time will this weather take from us?"

Karen watched as her husband lifted his coffee cup and rested it at cheek level as he bent his face over the mug and blinked several times. It was a strange habit of his to steam his eyelids. A stress reliever? Clearing his sinuses? She had never really known.

"I want to get you something this year," said Karen.

Jack put down his cup and looked at her sharply. "What?" he asked.

"A new coat."

"We won't have money for it."

"You need one," persisted Karen. "Yours is faded and worn, and far too thin."

"Who cares if it's faded? And I don't need a thicker one. This weather won't last. It can't, or we won't be able to afford anything for anyone."

Silence fell then, as they watched the snow continually drifting against the glass, and the sight seemed to add to the heaviness of their thoughts. Karen wished she could feel the carefree joy her children were now experiencing. She remembered playing with her own brothers and sister in the frequent snowfalls in Idaho. When she and Jack were teenagers and dating, they had an impromptu snowball fight on one of their excursions, laughing and then snuggling close in his car afterward to get warm.

Now it was time for their children to have fun, to treasure this much rarer opportunity for them.

But the longer this weather lasted, the more anxious she and Jack would both become, knowing Christmas was yet again slipping through their fingers—this year for quite an unexpected reason.

When their coffee cups were empty and there was no more to be had, they stood at the kitchen window as their kids had done and watched their children out on the big hill. The children weren't sledding, but what they were doing exactly was difficult to discern.

"Well," said Karen, trying to sound cheerful, "we can't do anything about the snow." She put her hand on Jack's arm. "Honey, let's go see what the kids are up to."

"Alright." Jack smiled down at her and gently moved a stray strand of silky hair from her face. "Let's watch them have their fun."

As Jack and Karen made their way from the house, their children sat at the top of the hill, conquerors of a stark world as they surveyed two distinct paths of beautiful, icy snow, the result of their labors.

"I want to go first," cried Hoodoo, standing up.

She grabbed for the cobbler pan, but Vinca pushed her hand back.

"Let Annie and Nate go first, and you and I will go next, okay?"

"Okay," she agreed reluctantly.

Hoodoo was envious of the shouts her sister and brother gave as they sped down. Annie spun around and around in the cobbler pan, trying to keep her feet up and gripping the sides with her fingers. She and Nate were almost in a small ditch along the bottom before they stopped. They came running back up, out of breath, and handed Vinca and Hoodoo the pan and hubcap. After Hoodoo arranged her bottom as best as she could in the metal pan, Annie cried, "Hold on!" and then gave her a push that made Hoodoo's heart lurch and then fall into her stomach as the world of field, forest, and dogs revolved around her dizzily.

Vinca giggled shrilly all the way down, an honor only given to great fun.

They had started the long haul up to hand off the hubcap and pan when Nate called out, "Hey, look! Mom and Dad are coming!"

"C'mon, quick!" he shouted.

Vinca and Hoodoo struggled back to the top through the small banks beside the sledding paths. Nate snatched the hubcap and cried, "Look at me, Mom and Dad!"

Violently, he shoved off the crest and went down with amazing speed, his high boyish laugh echoing in the woods until he hit a rock and was ejected from his sled. He got up hurriedly, rubbing his behind, and waved to his parents.

Jack and Karen walked hand in hand to the bottom of the hill and waited by the ditch as their children ran down to meet them.

"Isn't it great?" said Annie. "We made two awesome paths!"

"It was my idea," said Nate, folding his arms and giving his older sister a sidelong glare.

"Yes, I saw them from the house," answered Jack. "Good job."

"It's lots of fun!" remarked Hoodoo.

"I can see that. But Mom and I want you to get back up there."

To the top again they went, feeling ravenous from all the energy they had lost to the hill and the cold, but each sledded again several more times, sometimes skidding just to their parents' feet and laughing up at them with chapped cheeks.

Unable to resist, Jack snagged the hubcap when Annie got off of it and raced to the top, giving himself a push that was valiant but futile. He fell off into the snow halfway down as the kids laughed.

Brushing off his faded blue coat, he waved to Karen.

"C'mon, honey. Let me give you a push down the hill."

"No..." said Karen, giggling and shaking her head even though she was already starting forward to meet him.

"Ready?" he asked her after she had settled herself in a hubcap. She nodded. "Hold on!" He warned as he pushed.

Her long brown hair danced on the air. She went all the way down, so effective was Jack's push and her steering skills, until she tilted into the ditch. Her eyes shone as the kids ran to her, applauding. Hoodoo hugged and kissed her.

"That was really good, Mom," praised Nate, giving her back a pat of camaraderie.

The great hill could no longer compete with hunger and exhaustion, and the cold had remained decidedly unfriendly though the snow had ceased at last. The smoke filtering up through the chimney on the rooftop of the house beckoned them, and they started home.

Hoodoo scurried ahead of her mother and proudly pointed to her backside. "Look how wet my bottom is, Momma!"

"And frozen, too, I bet," replied Karen, giving it a good-natured smack.

Hoodoo hurried to catch up with Nate, trying to hold her wet jeans away from her legs with her fingers. Nate paused and pointed out some deer tracks, and they both knelt in the snow to look at them.

The little blue house, so plain and square, was a welcoming shelter from the chill. After Karen warned her children that she didn't want to see any snow inside, they danced noisily across the porch, knocking their feet against an old piano there to remove more. Then they marched inside where at last they were rewarded with mugs of homemade cocoa.

The Snowman

In the quiet of the early morning, Jack lay awake. He suffered from insomnia, but at this time of year it was not his worst enemy.

Disentangling himself from his wife's arms, he went out to the living room and watched the sparks glowing in the stove pipe that curved into the wall. He was afraid that pipe would grow too red one night and spread its heat into the structure, causing a fire he might catch too late.

This morning the old stove was emitting too little heat; his kids must be cold in their rooms. Quietly, he went into the kitchen and opened the back door to a slanting, wooden stoop. Switching on the outdoor light, he halted a few moments, surprised to see snow drifting down again through the uncommonly frigid air.

"No, *no*," he whispered to the indifferent, peacefully cascading crystals.

Worry was his worst enemy, and it came in winter more frequently than in other seasons, an unwelcome visitor who encamped stubbornly in his thoughts around the holidays.

Though he had gladly witnessed the joy it imparted to his children, this snow was not welcome anymore.

Jack and Karen Hoyle worked outdoors, in the vast hardwood forests of Tennessee, for their living. They needed good weather, or at the least tolerable conditions, in which to do their work, which consisted of harvesting some of Tennessee's native plants: bloodroot, sweet annie, ginseng, grapevine, and even briars. Ginseng was their best provider. The medicinal root was dug in the fall, its season monitored by the state. Price per ounce varied year by year, but hunting the unique and rare plants that hid among the undergrowth upon the forest floor and digging up their golden roots was a worthwhile endeavor. Fall was always an easier time for the Hoyle family.

In the winter, however, and for much of the rest of the year, Jack and Karen rolled grapevine and briar wreaths for a living, using clippers to trim and shape the vines, and tying them into bundles of ten to sell. It was meditative work in the heart of one of the state's most beautiful assets, its forests, but though wild grapevine grew in abundance in Tennessee, these wreaths that ended up in florists' shops decorated beautifully for festive homes or bare and expectant in a craft store were not the best providers. They were merely a means to get by.

Jack, an avid outdoorsman since a youth spent among the mountains, rivers, and pine forests of Idaho, enjoyed the work. He wandered over hills and hollows with his beautiful wife, whom everyone assumed by sight was a *hothouse flower*, far too lovely and delicate for such work. Despite her elegant bearing and slight build, however,

Karen kept up with Jack admirably as they walked for miles, worked hard, and talked freely.

They had only lost one day, but they needed to get back to that work right away. With the persisting cold and snowy conditions, however, the grapevine would still be too brittle and the trek too laborious to go in search of it.

Jack went around the house to retrieve more firewood from the front porch and sighed while gathering it up as he thought of how often in his life he had suffered anxiety about their livelihood.

His mind wandered back several years to when they had lived in Idaho and were expecting their fourth child, Heather, a surprise baby.

At that time Jack struggled to provide. For years he and his older brothers had gone from one temporary job to another in Idaho's faltering economy, from lumber mills to ranches to fruit orchards, in a constant effort to provide for their families with too little time and energy left to fall into discouragement. On the day Heather was born, Karen's mother was upset when she failed to reach Jack, but he was away looking for work. As it happened, on that day he finally found a good paying job with a powerline construction company.

For years after landing that job, he and his family traveled from state to state, and from project to project. His brothers came with him into the company and for a while they all moved together with their young families across the western United States, often pooling finances and renting homes together.

The work suited Jack, though it was tough and often dangerous, and the workday was long—light to light, dawn to dusk. From starting out as a common groundman, or grunt, he rose to lineman, foreman, and then to project engineer, in part because he taught himself Calculus in the evenings after grueling days. Eventually, he became a project manager.

In those years he had not worried about money, for he was handsomely paid, and his wallet was always full. But as his children grew and began to enter school, the act of uprooting his family every six months or so to travel to yet another project in yet another state became untenable.

Still, on nights like this when worry about finances blackened his heart, the idea that he should never have left the powerline nettled him.

But he had, and he left that lucrative job to chase a dream, one cherished from boyhood after he first learned to play a guitar. With a good deal of money saved and the gift of a Guild guitar from a good friend, he moved his family to Tennessee to become a songwriter, never imagining how hard it would be for a father of four to pursue such a career in which success was often based more on luck than upon talent. He played the nightclubs in Nashville religiously while Karen pitched his songs to music publishers.

Though eventually he was invited to perform his music on a respected morning radio show, the career he envisioned for himself in the Nashville music industry did not materialize. One music executive, who recognized his talent, advised him to abandon his family, to ship them off to live with relatives, so that he could collaborate with other songwriters inhabiting the basements of Music City.

Jack found the idea of abandoning his family deeply offensive, so, as the money saved from the years on the powerline slowly ran out, he went into business for himself painting houses, a skill he had learned from his father. He despised such work, even though affluent clients praised his skill and recommended him to their friends.

Then he met Barry Barton, an unusual man who sported an enormous gray beard, loved to smoke cigars, preferred to dress in military-style camouflage clothing, and seemed less interested in social norms and family obligations than he was in the Tennessee woods. Though he spoke little to women and ignored children, he communicated easily with other men in his hypnotic drawl.

With flowing and deliberate speech, he went on a long time, filling in his own regular pauses with a puff or two on a cheap cigar. He explained in detail to Jack that he was a buyer of nature's goods, reaped from the Tennessee landscape and its temperate climate. As Barry had talked on and on in that first meeting, Jack felt drawn to the prospect of laboring in the outdoors instead of at other people's homes.

It wasn't steady pay, but he didn't regret abandoning his buckets and brushes. Karen joined him in the woods, and their new work left him free to pursue songwriting.

Plus, he had found a good friend in Barry.

Nor did Jack really regret leaving the powerline. There had been little time left for his family while he pursued that career. After a stressful and exhausting day, many evenings he went to the bar to unwind with fellow linemen, and those men with whom he worked and drank were large figures in his life; he often stated that in their company, and in the tough daily grind of difficult and challenging labor, he had put away youth and become a man. But in those powerline days, his children awoke after he had gone to work and were often in bed before he came home. Karen raised their little ones almost without him.

As Jack carried his short stack of wood back into the house, he recalled how his surprise baby, whom he had nicknamed Hoodoo after a line in a Creedence Clearwater Revival song, hadn't had the opportunity to get to know him, and had once made it clear how little time she had spent in his presence.

It became a ritual, after they first moved to that little blue home at the end of a long Tennessee lane, for Jack to take each of his children out in turns to get a treat at the store.

When Hoodoo's turn came, she stood out on the front porch shaking her head at Jack with wide, anxious eyes.

"Can Momma come, too?" she asked.

"No," said Jack gently. "She needs to stay here with your sisters and brother. This is just for you and me—to spend some time together. Don't you want to go pick out something from the store?"

Again, Hoodoo shook her head vigorously, backing away. Karen stepped in and tried to convince Hoodoo in soothing tones to go with her dad.

"What treat would you like from the store, Hoodoo? A chocolate bar? A game of some sort?" Jack attempted next, kneeling before his little dark-haired girl.

Tears rolled down Hoodoo's face as she insisted, looking him in the eye, "I don't want to go. I want to stay with Momma!"

It had wrenched his heart.

As Jack blew on the coals in the old stove, his skin prickling as the heat met his cold appendages, he remembered how he felt that day, looking at the face of his youngest child who barely knew him, who didn't want to leave her mother's side to spend even half an hour with a stranger.

And then he suddenly remembered what Hoodoo had said to him the day before, holding his hand as they crossed the field. She had asked about Frosty and about the snow that brought him to life. He didn't get the chance to answer because of the snowball fight.

Hoodoo believed in snowmen like other kids believed in Santa Claus. She thought Frosty the Snowman was based on a true story and felt certain she might get to meet him or one of his cousins if the snow was right one winter day.

Jack lay back in his dilapidated recliner and put the footrest up, then folded his arms on his chest and imagined what he would create for

Hoodoo as he drifted off to sleep, one eye winking now and then at the old wood-burning stove.

In the morning, as she made coffee in the kitchen, Karen saw her husband walking home across the field and wondered where he had gone so early. Not for more wood. His arms were empty.

She met him at the door with a cup of coffee and inquired with a smile, "No wood? Just felt like some fresh frigid air?"

"I have a surprise for Hoodoo," he replied with a twinkle, his strange pale eyes alight with excitement.

Jack's youngest sat at the dining room table with quickly cooling Malt-o-Meal cereal before her, facing three beloved maple trees that waved their naked, snowy arms at her through the window. She turned and looked as her dad approached, her gaze less focused than usual, though it was not due to the brightness of the whitewashed world outside the window. Jack wondered again if she might need glasses and wondered, too, how they would pay for them if she did.

"Hoodoo, get your coat," Jack said, kneeling next to her. "I want to show you something in the woods." He stood as she dashed off to her room. "C'mon, everybody. Let's go for a walk!"

Vinca laid aside her book with regret and went to grab her winter things.

"What are you going to show us in the woods, Dad?" Nate asked, bent over Jack's shoulder as he watched him rearrange some logs in the stove.

"It's a surprise for Hoodoo," Jack whispered back.

"Oh."

Annie, hands extended over the woodstove as her long straw-colored hair nearly grazed its surface, glanced at Hoodoo skipping back down the hall and then shrugged at Nate.

"What is it, Daddy? What do you want to show me?" Hoodoo pestered ceaselessly while they made their way across the cornfield.

Jack's only response was to smile and say, "Just wait and see."

When they reached the first vanguard of trees Jack turned to her, bent down and said softly, "Hoodoo, there's a snowman in these woods, and I want you to meet him. I think this snow is just right for him to come to life. Are you ready?"

Hoodoo's deep brown eyes were wide as she nodded, excited but fearful as she held her dad's hand. The family broke through the brush at the edge of the forest, and a few minutes later they came upon the gentleman of snow leaning against a sturdy old maple in a small clearing.

He was a plain but well-rounded fellow. He had pebble eyes and a triangular piece of bark for a nose, the usual stick arms and a smile composed of more pebbles. There were stone buttons down his middle, but he wore no scarf or top hat, nor even a stocking cap. Hoodoo did not hold the lack of festive apparel against him. Still, he wasn't moving, and she hesitated.

"I think we should all dance around him," said Jack, as he handed Hoodoo an old stocking cap to place on the snowman's head. "Like the children do in the movie. We can sing 'Frosty the Snowman'."

Hoodoo's siblings didn't utter a word to indicate their feelings about the puerile thing they were about to do. Vinca was old enough to understand the need for her cooperation, and her face was passive. Annie studied Hoodoo's face for any hint of skepticism as a subtle smile played on her own face. Nate, however, rolled his eyes as they began to circle the ice man as a family, hand-in-hand and singing—Hoodoo at the top of her lungs—"Fraaah-sty the Snoooww-man...was a jol-ly, hap-py sooouul..."

They paused at the end of the song, and the woods were quiet once more. The snowman didn't move or talk or change his expression as Hoodoo stared at him expectantly.

"Ask him questions, see if he answers," said Jack, slowly retreating behind his youngest. "Don't be shy, Hoodoo!"

Hoodoo cleared her throat and took baby steps toward the humble snowman, watching for any movement.

"Hi...uh, hi." She looked back at her dad who nodded encouragingly. Then Hoodoo intoned, "I'm Heather. Are you Frosty?"

She sucked in a breath noisily, anticipating.

"No, no," the snowman answered in a man's wavering tenor. Then he laughed quietly. "But I know Frosty. We're good friends."

Hoodoo clapped her hands and jumped up and down.

"You are alive!"

"Well, of course I am! It's the snow."

"I know; this is magic snow! It sparkles with all the different colors. Do you live at the North Pole?"

"Sometimes," he answered in his strange yet familiar voice. "But at other times I visit children like you."

Hoodoo beamed at him as he continued to lean against the tree and clasped her hands in delight.

"I love you so much, Mr. Snowman, and I hope that you will come see me every time it snows," she said. She stepped closer to him as she continued, "Can you tell Santa to let Frosty come, too? I like his top hat, the magic one! Do you know how often magic snow falls? Is it only around Christmas?"

Again, the snowman gave his gentle laugh.

"Well, Christmas is a special time of year. A lot of wonderful things happen at Christmas. As for Frosty, well...I'll see what I can do."

"Please tell him to come," said Hoodoo. "Oh, but I forgot! What's your name?"

But the friendly snowman had no chance to give his name to Hoodoo, for suddenly Nate blurted out in exasperation, "Heather! *Come on*! He's not alive. *It's just Dad*!"

She froze, and then she turned to look at her father's face. His eyes held an odd look, as if he had been caught; his mouth was slightly ajar.

And she understood. Of course, of course it was her dad. That was why he stood behind her as she addressed the snowman; that was why the voice was strangely familiar. The truth always makes sense once realized, and it took only a quick moment for Hoodoo to realize it. She sobbed as she turned away from the false and lifeless snowman.

Karen grabbed her youngest child in a hug, whispering words of comfort.

Jack hovered nearby, motionless like his snowman, his face crestfallen.

Nate approached as Hoodoo's face was still buried in Karen's embrace. He patted her back awkwardly a couple of times and said softly, "Sorry, Hoodoo. I just... I... I'm sorry."

As he passed by his dad, Nate added, "Sorry, Dad," before turning away to kick through the snow.

Jack knelt by Hoodoo.

"Hoodoo, I had another day off because of the weather, and I wanted to give you a magical memory of this snowfall, but I guess I didn't do it right. I'm sorry."

The forest, along with everything in it, went quiet for a long moment. Then Hoodoo pulled away from Karen and encircled her dad's neck with her arms.

"It's okay, Daddy," she whispered.

Leaving the woods behind, the Hoyle family trudged back across the cornfield over the snowy terrain that now appeared impervious to childhood fancy. Hoodoo sniffled and wiped her wet cheeks with cold, stiff hands. Karen walked with her but glanced back at her husband and recognized well the expression etched on his face. It had been a good idea that had gone awry. She knew that the experience of that morning was worse for him than for Hoodoo.

Grapevine Wreaths

The kids returned to school on Wednesday, but their disappointment when they saw the snow melting on the ground and dripping above the porch was assuaged by anticipation of Christmas vacation. Small patches of snow glistened by the lane, mourning their own demise, when Jack drove them to the end of the lane to catch the bus.

On school mornings, Jack always said, "God bless and keep you," to his children, adding that they should remember their Heavenly Father and strive to please Him that day.

When the bus came down the hill on Spann Road, the children hugged Jack and ran out of the warm car and into the bus's heated interior.

Jack and Karen ate breakfast, then drove to a wooded area outside White Bluff to roll wreaths. With homemade denim lunch sacks slung over their shoulders that contained grilled cheese sandwiches, water bottles, and clippers, they ventured deep into the woods. The rich brown grapevines curled affectionately about the oak, maple, and hickory trees, and as they spied them, hope returned to Jack and Karen. Breathing hard from the trek, they each drew deeper breaths of relief.

They pulled on their work gloves, and Jack tested the wild vines and then yanked, bringing them to the ground, parting them from old trees that had become attached to new friends. To a small clearing he dragged these vines full of possibility, and Karen began to roll them against her stomach. Eventually Jack joined her, the thick vines snaking along the forest floor around them.

Winter brooded above the trees, and Karen and Jack found that their patch of sunlight was disloyal as the large, though naked, limbs of the trees cast their shadows about with the wind.

"Brrrrr," said Karen, shivering. Her delicate frame was hidden beneath layers of flannel, sweater and jean, but this protection from the elements was not what she wished it to be.

Jack looked up, his hands still deftly spinning a wreath as the grapevine at his feet leapt up to meet them with each turn.

"It's a weird winter, colder than usual," he acknowledged. "But, watch, it'll get back to normal by Christmas."

Karen nodded. "I'd be alright if it wasn't for this wind… brrr!"

Jack's thoughts were already on other things. "We have a bit of money still—if we can work hard and fast, we'll make the rent. Then we'll have ten or fifteen dollars apiece—if we're lucky—to spend on each of the kids." He glanced up from his wreath to meet his wife's face. "Or perhaps we could ask Mr. Adams for an extension."

Karen looked over at her husband without making a reply, and both looked down at their work. They had asked for rent extensions too many times already.

Jack tossed another finished wreath onto the pile. "There's Christmas dinner, too, and we need other groceries as well. The ham will be the most expensive thing, and the rest of our dinner will cost some, too." He hesitated, while Karen watched his expression, for his tone was gradually becoming more stressed. "We're going to cut it pretty close," he continued. "We won't be able to get anything for each other. I hate it that I can never give you even a simple piece of jewelry, certainly nothing like what I used to give you when I worked on the powerline."

"I'd rather have you home more," said Karen. "And the kids are far better off spending time with you than having things to get bored with."

Jack was silent, and Karen went on tentatively, "You need some things, and you haven't had anything new in a while, not even socks. I would love to get you a nice shirt at least. You don't need it, but you could use it."

"Yes, I could use it, but I don't want anything to interfere with the children's Christmas this year. *Nothing.* If we can't get anything for each other, well, then we can't. But the kids are going to have something."

"I'm worried about them, too," said Karen tersely.

"I know," replied Jack, irritated, clipping a wreath with his pliers. "So let's just aim for that, and whatever else we can do is icing on the cake."

They fell into a moody silence. Christmas, with all its supposed holly jollies, for a couple with a large family and a small bank account, was one of the most stressful times of year.

Karen loved their Christmas traditions: the live tree, the decorating with simple ornaments, the meal she cooked and enjoyed preparing, and the carols Jack played on his guitar. As for the presents, she imagined it would be hard enough to find the perfect gift for each child if money were no object, but when there was little money to spend, the challenge increased a hundredfold. They did their best with what they had, finding some little trinket related to that thing for which each child truly wished.

Jack began talking about ideas for each of their kids, and Karen silently prayed that their children would get what they wanted this year, a good Christmas, but as the one who managed the bills, she didn't know how it could be done in so little time. She and Jack soon began to talk about less wistful subjects: the bills due that month and those coming in January that preyed upon both of their minds.

Just past midday they took their lunch break, sitting close to one another on the trunk of a fallen tree in the clearing.

The significant pile of wreaths near them buoyed them up. Work would have gone better had the cold not been so fierce, making their fingers curl for warmth, growing stiff. Still, hope was found in that mound of wreaths that was soon to be lashed together in bundles.

They ate quickly and returned to work, to ward off the cold with exercise as well as to make a living. Four more hours of good light were ahead of them, and they were not going to waste that precious time.

While Jack and Karen labored in the deep woods, driven to produce as much as possible that day, miles away from them their children got off the bus at the end of the lane and began the walk home.

The nearly mile-long lane, with its hills and curves and overhanging trees, felt endless on such afternoons. To make it worse there was a steady wind as the kids made their way between the large, sloping field full of cows and barren blackberry bushes on their right, and the bluff on their left. That bluff descended into a ravine wild with vegetation where the creek ran over beautiful, large rocks that glistened with emerald moss in spring. The sound of that water, so musical and inviting on warmer days, made them shiver now.

Hoodoo, nevertheless, gave a shout as she exited the school bus and took off running. Annie glanced back at the windows of the bus to see if her friends had noticed the embarrassing behavior of her little sister. The wind eventually thrust the cries back in Hoodoo's throat, and unable to maintain a jog with burning lungs, she turned back to walk with her siblings.

Nate and Annie often walked the whole way home in competition. Annie felt it was her natural right, being older, to walk in front of her brother, and Nate tried to outpace her, because he didn't want to get beaten to the house by a girl. He smirked, and she scowled as they jockeyed for position the whole way home every afternoon.

When they had to walk to the bus stop in the morning, however, on the way *to school*, the competition appeared to be who could go the slowest.

Today, Nate didn't seem to care. He stared glumly at the dirt beneath his feet and kicked a stone now and then with such ferocity that some of them pinged against innocent trees.

"What's the matter with you?" Vinca asked, irritated.

"Christmas. It's less than a week away."

"So? Don't you like getting out of school? Don't you like presents, Grinch?"

"I like presents," said Nate, kicking another stone violently into the ravine. "But we aren't going to get any."

"How do you know?" asked Annie, her tone fearful.

"Like I said," Nate answered, "it's less than a week away, isn't it?"

Vinca reflected and acknowledged, "He may be right. Mom and Dad couldn't work because of the snow, and I heard them talking about the rent before bed."

"See?" said Nate. "And now Dad will get depressed, too."

There was silence as they crossed the dirt-covered culvert over their beloved creek, the center of their summertime adventures. Trees crowded its banks and bent over its undulant surface, as if enthralled by the endless melody of its passage.

Normally, this was the point where the Hoyle children quickened their pace, for it was more than halfway to home. But today their thoughts slowed them down, wondering what Christmas would hold for them this year.

As they walked onward, the creek curved to follow the lane several yards away on their left, but now the ground had flattened out there, and was covered with a riot of tangled young trees. To their right, there was a second field that abutted the creek and its sylvan companions, more level than the one at the top of the lane. This was the field that eventually encountered the big hill, hidden from them by a shoulder of woodland. Home was around the next bend. Reuben appeared, barking a low greeting. Mandy, hearing her humans, had already come down the lane to greet Annie with great enthusiasm.

"Dad really does get depressed," said Annie as she scratched Mandy's ear.

Hoodoo continued skipping down the lane, blithely ignoring dire forecasts.

"Alright," said Vinca. "He does at first, yes. But not when Christmas actually comes around, and we're all decorating the tree together and Mom's making pies. Dad likes that. Regardless, we'll have ham for dinner and Mom's sweet potato casserole."

"Yum, ham!" Nate said, as his thoughts turned to the needs of his stomach.

"And stuffing, too," said Annie. "That's my favorite."

"And parker house rolls!" shouted Hoodoo.

"And we've had presents before, anyway, lots of them," Vinca reminded them all. "Remember your train set, Nate?"

"Yeah, that's still my favorite. But that was a while ago."

"Well, we might get something this year. We might," repeated Vinca, more to encourage herself, perhaps, than her siblings. She retrieved the house key from the very back of the mailbox that was opposite the driveway.

"I wish I could have some new clothes," said Annie. "But I guess I'd rather have some drawing supplies."

"I want a Barbie doll," said Hoodoo, still skipping as she followed Vinca up the driveway. "And I need new pannies."

"Don't you mean panties, Hoodoo?" asked Annie scornfully. "What do you want, Nate?"

"A G.I. Joe," he answered, a small note of hope in his tone.

"Mom and Dad never get presents," said Vinca as she bent to unlock the door. "They never get anything. I wonder what they would want..."

The door opened; they all pushed inside, including the dogs, as the kids thought a moment about what parents wish for. Yet as the residual heat from the old stove met them and then seemed to dissipate entirely as the cold rushed at their backs, such perplexing thoughts vanished, and they were again contemplating their own desire for Christmas presents.

Barry Barton

Barry Barton's large house with its broad porch was on a quiet street at the edge of the town of White Bluff. On Thursday evening, after another long day of rolling wreaths, Jack and Karen pulled up the climbing driveway past the huge oak that lined his lane, the house on their right. It had once been white, but years of neglect had invited gray and yellow to dominate its old siding.

Jack and Karen parked their car in the rutted yard to their left that spread away toward Barry's neighbor with no discernible border. Barry was in the shed, that served as his open-air office, at the end of the driveway. The line of people waiting to sell their wreaths was shorter than usual, and Jack was grateful; they needed to get to the grocery store for their kids' dinner.

Barry was not known for moving people along. He took a leisurely half hour with each of his favorite sellers unless they could convince him nicely that they were in a hurry. Few possessed that talent, and none wanted to offend their buyer, so most did not escape.

After Jack had taken twine from his trunk and stacked his cache of wreaths ten high, securing them with the knotted twine on two sides, he saw that the line tonight was moving along quickly.

Again, Jack was grateful. It had been a long day in the cold. It would be nice to get home.

Barry glanced up from writing a check for a huge, bearded fellow who might have been mistaken for Bigfoot under the right conditions. He waved to Jack with a smile, his cigar still dangling from the corner of his mouth, but then Barry dropped his hand, and a sad expression came into his already melancholy brown eyes that nearly met his beard. He took a puff or two on his cigar and turned back to the bearded fellow to say a few more words.

Puzzled, Jack wondered if Barry's kids were unwell or if he had had another fight with his wife, Sharon. Jack didn't like Sharon particularly—she was a person who always appeared affronted, as if she weren't receiving her due from life—but he nevertheless felt sorry for any normal woman attached to Barry. Barry's idea of a romantic getaway involved camping in the Tennessee woods or down by some slow-moving, muddy river.

Jack noticed that each person who passed him after selling their wreaths had an unhappy expression that ranged from disgruntled or disappointed to downright angry. Many were studying the checks in their hands. Had Barry dropped his prices for some reason? Would he do that? Christmas was a week away. Perhaps Barry was short this year and trying to save for his own kids' gifts. Jack became apprehensive.

Finally, he stood just outside the shed, one foot planted on the steps, trying not to eavesdrop on Barry's low conversation with the guy ahead of him who was responding to Barry in irritated tones. Jack, filled with impatience to learn the reason for all the discontent, once more cursed the snow that had taken three working days from them.

When he stepped up at last, Barry asked as usual, "How many ya bring, Jack?"

"Two hundred and forty," Jack said. "All fourteen inch."

"A'right." Barry punched numbers into his calculator. Then he looked up with that doleful expression that worried Jack. "Family a'right? Doin' good?"

Jack breathed deeply and said, "They're good. The kids enjoyed the snow even if Karen and I wished we could have been out rolling. How is your family?"

Barry settled back, puffed on his cigar, and began, "A'right, I s'pose. Michelle got the flu las' week. Told her to res' and eat some oranges— weren't cheap, them oranges I got—but her momma took her to the doctor to get med'cine. When I was a boy, my brothers and me jus' toughed it out, ya know? No doctors. No pills. Nature. Nature knows what we need to feel good. Ya want a cigar, Jack?"

Jack took one out of the package Barry held out, and he picked up the lighter from Barry's desk and lit it. The cigars were cheap and harsh; Jack had smoked far better when he worked on the powerline, but there was no money for those now.

The act of smoking a cigar, even one as terrible as those Barry kept in stock, reminded him of different times, and the smoke created an illusion of warmth to distract Jack somewhat from the cold that was inching deeper between the layers of his worn shirts.

"Thanks, Barry," he said. Then he waited and watched as Barry studied the number on the calculator and wrote out the check. When he handed it to Jack, Jack was startled. He knew quite well how much he and Karen should have made for their bundles of wreaths. This was more.

"Uh, Barry…" he began.

Barry waved his hand through the smoke of the shed in a dismissive way.

"Jack, I don't know how ya'll are doin'," began Barry, leaning back to gaze at Jack with that lost puppy dog expression that made Jack want to yell at him to spit out whatever bad news he had, "but I got some… well… not good news, I'm sad to say. Told my other rollers, too, and it hasn't been a good night, I'll tell ya. I sure hope it won't put ya in a bind, and I can't tell ya how sorry I am. It's nothin' I can help, ya see."

Hard lines took over Jack's naturally stern face. He swallowed some of the corrosive smoke from the cigar, making him cough.

Barry continued through Jack's coughing fit, "I can't buy any more wreaths for a bit," he stated flatly. "Wish I could, but I'm swamped. Adam Riggs down the road here jus' opened up his business abou' a month ago and stole some o' my bes' customers. Folks keep bringin' me business, and I keep on buyin' though I shouldn't." He paused and shook his head. "Florists and craft stores have started contractin' with the bigger buyers. Riggs took two o' my biggest customers before the snow. No loyalty at all! He dresses sharp and talks pretty - don't look like no woodsman at all! But he charms 'em and steals business even though he ain't been ten feet inside o' the woods."

He drew deeply on his cigar, his expression no longer doleful but angry. Jack stared at him and then looked down at the check in his hand before he heard Barry begin again.

"I ain't had much luck sellin' what I got. I got too many, Jack. And I'm runnin' outta money to buy."

The two men stared at each other in silence for a few moments. Jack had lost all interest in the cigar, but Barry still puffed his slowly from the side of his mouth, blowing smoke now and again.

"So you can't take anymore at all?" said Jack, his expression intense.

"Nah, I can't," said Barry, meeting his friend's gaze. "I'd like to, but I jus' can't. That don't mean business won't pick up," he added hastily. "It jus' ain't good right now."

Jack forced himself to say the words, "Then you couldn't afford to take these tonight."

"Hey, no, that's fine," said Barry quickly, sitting up and pushing back Jack's hand holding out the check. Then he stated again, sadly, "But I've run outta money to buy with, like I told ya." After a pause he looked straight up at Jack's face and said slowly, "I hope it hasn't messed up yer Christmas, Jack."

"That's not important," Jack said. "But I need to make rent and feed my kids. Will you be able to buy again, you think?"

As Jack asked the question, he was thinking about all the houses he had painted when they first moved to Tennessee—work he hated, but that now seemed his only option to provide for his family.

"In January, maybe I can wrangle it." Barry's tone was apologetic. "I might have to sell my inventory for less to a larger buyer, but I'll do it if need be. Jus' not to that damn Adam Riggs," he added vehemently. Then he settled back again in his swivel chair before saying earnestly, "I'd hate to lose ya and Karen to another buyer. Yer my bes' rollers. But I know ya gotta do what ya gotta do, no hard feelins. But I'll buy again, Jack. Just gimme a couple weeks to get some customers back."

"Alright; I'll have to count on that," said Jack shortly, staring hard up at the racoon furs hanging from the ceiling of Barry's shed and thinking about the kids' sunken Christmas with suppressed anger.

"If ya want, I can lend ya money to get by. Wouldn't be much, but I can do it."

Jack looked back down, and Barry found it hard to meet those intense, strangely pale eyes of his friend's without flinching, especially because of the expression they now held.

Then Jack looked again at the check before shoving it deep in his pocket. "Thanks, Barry. We'll get through until you buy again." Barry stood up, and they shook hands as Jack added, "I've got to go. Karen and I need to pick up groceries."

He turned and walked down the steps.

Barry called after him, "If ya get in a bind, I'm righ' here. Just gimme a call. I'll be here, Jack."

Jack stopped and turned to face his friend. "Thanks, Barry. Goodnight.'

"Goodnight. And Merry Christmas!"

Jack forced a smile that did nothing to soften his features in the harsh light from Barry's shed.

"Merry Christmas."

Then he put a hand on Karen's shoulder and guided her to their car where he opened the door for her. Karen flinched when he slammed it behind her. His face told her something was very wrong, and with every moment that passed, her stomach knotted more tightly as her anxiety grew to discover what it was.

She remained quiet as he started the old sedan and backed it out, the cast of his face alarming as he turned to look out the rear window. He yanked the wheel to guide them onto the street and the tires spun on the gravel before gripping and pulling forward.

As they headed to the grocery store, Jack rested his left elbow against the window, his head cocked that way. His hand methodically controlled the wheel as he drove too fast for Karen's comfort. His posture was one of defeat.

"You forgot to buckle your seatbelt," Karen said softly, and Jack shoved the catch roughly into the buckle.

"There's another Christmas shot to hell," he said.

"What happened?" asked Karen urgently. "What did Barry say to you?"

"He can't buy more wreaths, that's what. *Forget Christmas.* Rent, groceries—we don't have enough. He wrote me a check for two hundred dollars. That's it. And it's more than he should have given us. But even with the measly bit we already have, it's just not enough. And God only knows when Barry can buy again. We might just starve!"

"Why won't he buy more wreaths?" Karen asked in a low tone.

"More buyers. More competition. He's lost some business... I don't know. I don't know..."

Karen felt confused as well as frightened. They had been selling to Barry for years, everything from bloodroot to ginseng to briar wreaths. This had never happened.

Jack pulled sharply into the grocery store parking lot, parked in a space under the blue and red sign that hung over its entrance, and turned off the car in disgust.

"I wish I'd never left the powerline," he said, glaring out the window.

Karen sighed. Those were damning words to Hoyle household peace. When Jack uttered those words, he was beyond discouragement, heading down a dark tunnel toward despair and regret at an alarming speed, and it was never easy to draw him back out of it. All she could do was ride it out and withstand as best she could his self-condemning moods.

In truth, Karen at times missed the luxuries she and Jack had been able to afford during his powerline days, but she wished he could have seen how disruptive that career was to their family life and how lonely she had often felt at that time—many days feeling like a single mother to their four children.

In financial terms, their life in Tennessee was harder than it had ever been when he worked construction, but it was so much fuller in every other way.

Yet she realized that there was more behind that utterance, too. It concealed the great specter of disappointment that haunted Jack when he dwelled on the fact that he had not yet achieved his dream of being a singer-songwriter in Nashville, that he had not succeeded when there was yet money from the powerline to invest in hope. His Guild guitar sat in the corner of the living room at the end of every long day, an ever present, now often silent partner in frustrated dreams. Jack still pursued Nashville in spurts when they had more money—especially in the fall during ginseng season—but he allowed the dream to die anew whenever clothes for the kids or bills ate up their resources.

And whenever finances became a profound cause of frustration, Jack remembered the money he had made while traveling the West with a powerline construction company, and the success he'd known in climbing its ranks as well as its massive electrical poles. At such times his life felt like failure simply because he was poor.

Aware of all these shadows in her husband's thoughts, Karen leaned over and touched his thigh lightly.

"We'll find something. We'll figure it out. I can call around to other buyers, honey."

Jack shook his head but said nothing.

"And I'll call our landlord," she went on. "I'll ask for an extension."

"I'll have to go back to painting," Jack said dejectedly. "But who will want their house painted in the week before Christmas?" Again, he shook his head. "There will be nothing for the kids. Nothing."

"Honey, it'll be alright," Karen told him. "The kids don't really need presents. That's not what Christmas is about, anyway."

"I know that, Karen. But I would like to be able to do something for my children. I don't even make enough to buy them new clothes as often as they need them."

"You're a good father," said Karen, but she removed her hand from his thigh. "You are always there when they need you, always talking to them and playing games with them. They love spending time with you. They would not have that if you were still working on the powerline. And they don't need presents this year. We'll...we'll do something else that's fun."

"Then you tell them, Karen. You tell them."

They sat in silence, each staring through the windshield at the storefront, neither moving to get those groceries they needed so badly.

"Do you know how this makes me feel?" Jack asked finally.

"Yes, I know; I know."

Another heavy silence ensued, but then Jack stirred himself and pulled the car keys from the ignition.

"We'd better sign this check and go get those kids some supper," he said.

God Will Provide

The Hoyle kids heard the car pulling up the driveway and froze where they were, listening, crowding near each other by the old stove in the living room. They glanced at one another nervously and each quickly found a spot on the couch or in a chair.

Every time they fought when their dad and mom were away, yelling and pointing fingers while threatening siblings with creative tortures, they tried to hide it by breaking up at the sound of the car to sit down.

But somehow—*somehow*—their dad always knew. He looked around at them with that piercing and intimidating gaze and began to ask knowing questions. Half-jokingly, half-seriously, they suggested that God was the one feeding their dad information, since He was the only witness to their bickering.

They didn't realize that sitting around like placid angels betrayed them.

This evening when the door opened, neither of their parents seemed to notice their attitudes of peaceful contemplation, nor did their dad ask as they expected, "Alright, what were you kids fighting about?"

As he set some groceries on the table, he simply stated gruffly, "There are things in there to snack on until your mom gets dinner ready."

They all caught the dark look on his face as he headed out the door to fetch the other bags.

"What's wrong with Dad?" Vinca asked as her mother began unpacking the groceries.

"Oh, nothing," Karen replied, sighing.

"He looks mad," said Annie.

"He'll tell you kids about it when he comes back in," their mother answered, her pretty features drawn in tight lines.

The four kids looked at one another, their argument forgotten as they unified in concern. Their dad was like the ocean tide of their family. When Jack felt good and loved life, so did his wife and kids, buoyed upon the wave crests of his good moods, basking in the frequent sunny smiles that so marvelously softened the sternness of his face. But when he was down, all felt inexorably dragged back into the sea with him, finding it hard to be happy and hopeful when Jack's face was set rigidly against life's upsets.

The kids sat again, tense as they watched their father bring in the last sacks of the groceries, nervously munching their snacks because they were too hungry to let stress deprive them of food.

Jack closed and locked the front door, and then sat down in his dilapidated recliner, shutting his eyes for several minutes as his children took turns staring at him. Then he leaned forward in his chair, called for his wife, and said, "Kids, I need to talk to you about something."

Vinca's heart sank as she recalled the conversation she and her siblings had had on the walk home, and she scooped up Tommy where he lounged by the woodstove, holding him close for moral support.

She was sure she knew what her dad was going to say and was determined not to let her disappointment show too much.

"Kids, I know I said we were going to have Christmas... Christmas with presents this year," Jack paused as he saw the shadows overtaking his kids' faces at these words. He swallowed and looked down. Hard as it was, he had to finish. They should know the truth well before the arrival of Christmas morning.

"Things have happened that are beyond our control... with work... and we can't afford presents." He shook his head with sadness in his pale eyes. "We just can't swing it. I know how disappointing this is, but there's nothing your mother and I can do. We have to worry about food and bills now."

The children were silent for many moments. Vinca felt the sting of the truth though the realization had struck some minutes before. Annie started thinking about what she would tell her friends at school when they stood around boasting of their endless, luxurious presents; she would just make stuff up, she resolved. Nate angrily watched G.I. Joes march before his eyes with all their gear and their awesome forts, parading away into other boys' hands and toy boxes. Hoodoo looked sadly at her father, not sure whether she felt most sorry for him or for herself, deprived of a beautiful Barbie doll.

"Can we still have a tree?" Hoodoo asked.

"Of course," said Karen, though Hoodoo's words stung her heart. "I promise you we'll decorate the tree and make it the prettiest one we've ever had."

"Yes, we'll get our tree, Hoodoo," said Jack, leaning back in his chair to avoid the expressions on his children's faces that caused him pain. "And we'll do our best for Christmas dinner, too."

Please, please let us still have ham, thought Nate.

The house was silent as Karen prepared supper. Annie whispered to her as she stood at her elbow near the stove, her siblings crowding around their mother, too, who felt like a haven in times like these.

"Mom?"

"Yes, Annie."

"We have to get the Secret Santa gifts for the kids at school."

Karen whirled and stared at Annie, a large spoon dripping in her hands.

"*What*? What do you mean? Why hasn't anybody told me?"

"We did," said Nate. "We have to get them, Mom. We all picked names out of a sack in our class. Whatever name we get, we have to bring a present for that person. That's the way they work it."

"I don't have to get a present," Vinca assured her mother. "They only do that in the elementary school. I'll just make Christmas cards for all my friends."

"Do you three absolutely have to get them?" Karen inquired urgently. "Can't you explain to your teachers?"

Annie, Nate, and Hoodoo all glanced around desperately. None of them wished to have that conversation on the day of the present exchange.

"Alright," said Karen, but her widened eyes defied this acceptance. "How much do you have to spend?"

"My teacher said not to spend more than five dollars," Annie told her.

"We only have to spend a couple dollars," said Nate.

"Go, sit down on the couch. I'll have to think about this and tell your dad somehow."

"Honey," Karen spoke up hesitantly during dinner, "I... I'd forgotten. The kids... well, they're supposed to buy gifts for classmates for their school parties tomorrow." She paused, seeing the look coming over Jack's face, and added hastily, "Just one child whose name they pulled from a hat. It doesn't have to be much, only a dollar or two."

"*We can't afford a dollar or two.*"

The kids froze in their chairs, looking down at the tabletop, feeling badly for their mother but grateful they had not broken the news.

"I know, honey. I told the kids they will just have to explain to their teachers. I can call them myself if I need to."

The kids saw stress harden Jack's face, fissuring it into fine lines.

"Who's stupid idea is this?" he demanded. "My kids can't have Christmas this year, but I have to make sure other people's kids do?"

"No—no, honey. I will call their teachers tomorrow. Don't worry about it."

"Daddy, we all get presents from the other kids, too," muttered Hoodoo, close to tears.

Jack looked at his youngest girl and then at Nate and Annie.

"*Fine*," he said. "Everyone grab your coats, and let's go get these stupid presents before the store closes."

He stood, as did Karen. She leaned over to him, speaking in low tones, "No, it's alright. We can't afford it."

"Well, we're getting them," responded Jack brusquely. "Let's hope it leaves us money for food." He looked over to where their kids stood huddled by the front door, pulling on jackets. "Are you kids ready? Out to the car then!"

On the drive to town, the heat generated by their old vehicle floated around their bodies like a ghost without ever truly warming them. The heavy clouds in the dark sky aimed to sink their spirits further, and the many trees that lined the roadways—so beautiful in warmer seasons—rattled and sighed in the wind, bemoaning their present desolation.

It was close to nine when they pulled into the parking lot of the Kmart. Jack retrieved a ten-dollar bill and handed it to Karen.

"Please don't spend it all. We can't afford to waste a cent. These things don't need to be fancy. Whatever you can find."

"Are you coming in?"

"No. Vinca, go with your mother and help the other kids be quick about it," Jack said.

Jack shut off the car while he waited, not willing to waste gas to keep himself warm.

He was grateful when his family reemerged from the store half an hour later; the reappearance of his wife and children snatched him back from worried thoughts that gnawed at him far more ferociously than the cold.

Jack brought the car up near the front of the store, and everyone climbed in.

"Daddy, do you want to see what we got?" asked Hoodoo, innocently excited.

"Not tonight, Hoodoo."

Karen handed him fifty-four cents.

"That's the change," she said softly.

"I didn't expect to do better. It's okay."

He reached over and squeezed her hand.

"You don't have to worry about anything else tonight," Karen told him.

Jack gave no response to this, for there was a great deal to worry about.

The drive home was as gloomy as the one to the store, saving Hoodoo's excitement over the gift she had found. The headlights projected dully onto the pavement before them, and the tall, naked trees waved their spindly arms at the dark sky as if in desperate prayer. There was no comforting, understanding glow shed on them from above; the moon was absent, and the stars were all obscured.

The kids heard their mother ask, "How much money do we have left?"

"Not much," their dad responded. "We're still short on the rent, and we're going to need more groceries next week. We'll be broke soon if I can't find something to do." He sighed. "I really don't know what we're going to do."

He didn't think long before he thumped his fist against the steering wheel.

"Dammit! Dammit!"

Startled, no one spoke for several minutes.

"It'll be okay," Karen whispered. "We'll manage somehow. We'll find work."

"It's not going to be okay, Karen, and where are we supposed to find work?" Jack demanded, his voice raised. "Why did this happen in winter? The absolute worst luck for this to happen in winter. We have nothing!"

In the back seat, his three younger children contemplated Jack's words.

Feeling sick to her stomach, Annie wondered if the landlord would throw out her family before Christmas. Where would they go? Would the kids at school find out?

Arms tightly folded across his chest, Nate sat between his sisters, dismissing Christmas as the worst time of year.

Hoodoo sank deeper into the car seat, scared as she wondered why her family was upset lately about everything.

It was a shock to everyone else when Vinca said, "Dad, you said that God would always take care of us."

Karen looked at Jack, appealing to him to take his own words to heart, for, as Vinca stated, he had often spoken these words to them.

Jack returned no answer for a few moments. He inhaled deeply, breathed out, and said in a subdued voice, "You're right, Vinca. God will take care of us. But it's hard to wait and see how He plans to do that."

When they got home, Jack retrieved his battered black Bible from the shelf and read from Matthew, Chapter Six, to his family in his clear, authoritative voice that made Hoodoo think Jesus must have sounded like her dad when he spoke to the people:

Therefore take no thought, saying, What shall we eat? or, What shall we drink? or, Wherewithal shall we be clothed? For after all these things do the gentiles seek: for your heavenly Father knows that ye have need of all these things. But seek ye first the kingdom of God, and his righteousness; and all these things shall be added unto you. Take therefore no thought for the morrow: for the morrow shall take thought for the things of itself. Sufficient unto the day is the evil thereof.

When he closed the Bible in his hands, he looked around at his family, the family he loved mightily and for whom he needed a means to provide, and prayed silently, *"Lord, I believe, but help my unbelief."*

Karen watched her husband's tired face for several long moments in silence, her brown eyes luminous. When she got up, she kissed his bearded cheek and gestured to the children, shooing them toward the hall.

"It's time for bed. Hurry up and get ready."

A Garland

Annie, Nate, and Hoodoo held little paper bags in their hands containing a small toy for a child at school when their dad drove them to the end of the lane Friday morning to catch the bus. Jack frowned at the sacks; he could not help but feel resentment about the money taken from his family, though a meagre amount. The younger kids clutched them, hoping the gifts they received in return from classmates would be far better than anticipated if they would be the only ones received that year.

When Jack got home, Karen was rummaging through dusty cardboard boxes stuffed with papers, searching out the names of old clients for whom Jack had done painting work. They both knew they could not waste time in finding employment. They prayed for even a small job before Christmas.

After eight o'clock Karen began calling all the names that she had excavated, while Jack listened, discouraged, as time and again, clients informed her that they had no need of painting. Finally, however, a person was interested; she wanted her dining room painted for a big holiday gathering.

When Jack heard the name, his heart sank. This well-to-do woman was one of the pickiest he had ever met. As soon as a chosen color was on the wall, she decided that she didn't like it after all and wanted a different shade. Jack remembered buying quart after quart, rolling paint on with a grimace as the wealthy client watched over his shoulder. Once the work was done, he knew she would point out every single dot of paint that she perceived to be misplaced, and the touch-up work would cost him much in exasperation.

But there was no help for it, and when he heard Karen repeat that, yes, he could begin Saturday morning to finish in time for Christmas Eve—if the client knew what she wanted—he nodded his head in grim satisfaction.

The kids were surprised when the bus dropped them off, and their mother was there alone. Hoodoo hugged her hard and began to skip down the lane.

"It's Christmas vacation!" she shouted back at her mother and siblings, twirling, and she ran her hands over the needles of a few pine trees that grew on the right side of the lane as she passed them. When she slowed down to take her mother's hand, she asked, "Where's Daddy?"

"Your dad is consulting with a woman who wants her dining room painted. So we can pay bills," said Karen.

Hoodoo studied her momma's face.

"When will he be home?"

"Not until late probably."

"Okay. Look at my gift, Momma!"

Hoodoo was dangling a green and red plastic wreath ornament from her index finger.

"Very nice," said Karen with as much gaiety as she could muster, though she was thinking sadly of grapevine wreaths. "What did you get, Annie and Nate?"

They dug into their bags and brought out equally cheap gestures of the season, less pleased than Hoodoo with their bounty.

Jack did indeed come home late, weary and irritated.

"I remember now why I hate painting so much," he said, bending over to untie his work boots. When he sat up again, Karen handed him a plate of supper. "That woman did just what I expected. I went to the paint store three times, and I can only hope she sticks with the color we have now, though it's hideous—purple!"

Nate came and stood by his father, putting an arm over the back of the chair. "Dad, can we still get the tree tomorrow?"

Jack looked up at him, "I'm afraid not, son. I have to work tomorrow, painting this lady's house. But maybe we can get it on Sunday, okay?"

"Oh, okay." Nate returned to the table where he shoved the food around with his fork.

Saturday was a watery sunlit day. The sky was glazed a dull gray, and the sun shone languidly upon an equally dull earth. All of Mother Nature's plants were deprived of their glorious mantle, even the brilliant white one they had borrowed from Old Man Winter several days before. It drizzled.

Dressed in an old shirt and jeans spattered with flecks of paint, Jack kissed Karen, hugged his children and warned them to be good for their mother, and left early for a nice neighborhood in Dickson, about half an hour away, to paint a formal dining room for a finicky lady.

Without their father's presence the day was unbearably boring to Nate and Hoodoo—seasonless, too, without a tree in the corner of the living room. Vinca sat curled up in a chair with a book propped against her knee; that was her escape from a drab world devoid of Christmas prospects. Annie sketched on the unused side of her school papers, imagining surreal things for her own amusement.

Eventually, Nate and Hoodoo teased Sammy the cat with some string; he was very patient with their tactics and was always up for any game they devised, unlike his brother Tommy who was barely willing to tolerate the plethora of humans, except for Vinca, who surrounded him. Sammy eventually padded off to lie by Reuben who was a great source of warmth for the thin feline. Nate and Hoodoo then lined up army men in the gray dust by the woodstove, but it was far less fun to play indoors where there were no dirt clods to throw or straw forts to build.

Even Reuben and Mandy were listless. Reuben lay by the front door, his back against its cold surface, waiting for Jack's returning footstep.

Mandy nipped at Reuben's broad neck to get him to play, but, giving up, curled up at Annie's feet under the dining table and slept.

The kids paid no attention to the work their mother was doing until a strange popping noise led them into the kitchen. The electric skillet was on. Their mother grabbed the lid and handle, shaking the skillet back and forth.

"You're making popcorn," Annie said. "Why?"

"Well, I found some kernels this morning, and I thought we could make a garland for our tree," responded Karen. "It would be a nice way to pass the time until your dad gets back."

"We don't have a tree," Nate reminded his mom.

"Don't worry, Nate," she said, ruffling his thick, dark hair before pouring cream-colored clouds into a large bowl. "We'll get it soon, a big beautiful one. And then we'll have our garland ready to put on."

Annie poured more oil into the skillet, and Vinca refilled it with kernels from a mangled bag that had obviously been forgotten for some time.

Hoodoo tasted the popcorn.

"Ugh... it's stale!"

"That doesn't matter," said Karen. "Unless you keep snagging some."

"Momma, I haven't done anything," Hoodoo said as she watched her older sisters take over the popping.

"You can thread the needle for me if you want."

71

"But I can't see the hole in the needle."

"Then, I'll thread the needle and you can start the garland while we're waiting for this other batch to get done."

"Yay!"

Karen threaded a thick needle with a lengthy piece of thread, tying a large knot at the end. She demonstrated how to string the popped kernels of corn and handed it to Hoodoo.

Hoodoo's eyes kept wanting to cross as she concentrated on her task, and her tongue stuck out involuntarily from the side of her mouth in her effort to subdue and align the popcorn. Repeatedly, she held up the needle to display the popcorn dangling at the end of the thread for her mother and just as often she cried, "Ouch," when she pricked her fingers.

"Good work," said Karen. "But be careful with that needle."

Hoodoo relinquished the string of popcorn gladly from her aching fingers to Vinca who studied the shape of each piece of fluffy corn before placing it in proper order with its fellows on the garland. When Annie's turn came, she poked her fingers with the needle constantly, exclaiming sharply each time. Eventually, she dropped the garland in her lap and sucked at her thumb. Karen took it and covered the last bit of thread. She tied it off, threaded the needle again, and offered it to her son who had shown little interest in the project.

"Well, Nate? Want to help?"

"I guess so."

Not half the popcorn had been used, but Nate was intent on the work and covered a large section of garland before handing it to Hoodoo. No longer enamored with this craft, she estimated what a reasonable amount of effort might look like, far less than what her brother had done, before passing it to Annie.

The second section, now completely full, was tied to the first, and Vinca and Karen completed a third section by themselves before attaching it to the first two. The kids helped Karen lay it out across the living and dining room floor. It nearly reached from one wall to the other of the large rectangular space.

"Well, it's going to be beautiful on our tree," said Karen, gathering it up in her arms. "I used to love making popcorn garlands as a kid!"

She coiled it carefully on the table.

When Jack came home that evening, the kids and Reuben crowded around him at the door, but the Labrador managed to maneuver closest to Jack and followed him to the couch. As soon as Jack sat down, Reuben sprang into his lap like a puppy.

"Alright, Reuben! Down!" said Jack hoarsely, laughing though he was being crushed by more than ninety pounds of dog.

When Reuben had obeyed, sitting by Jack's feet on the floor and looking up at him, panting and smiling, Jack reached into his pocket and handed Karen a money order.

"Picked that up for the rent on the way home," he said. "She paid me fifty percent today, and I should be done by Monday evening."

"A funny thing happened at the store when I got that," Jack added after removing his work boots, pointing to the slim paper representing most of their funds. "I was headed into the store, and as I approached the entrance, I noticed an older man crossing the pavement out of the corner of my eye. It was chilly, and he was wearing only a short-sleeved T-shirt. He was thin as a rail, and his arms were tight against his chest. I was feeling sorry for him as I went through the doors, and then I paused. I realized I should have given him my jacket. So, I went straight back out, taking off my coat as I went..." Jack looked from his wife's face to those of his children who were close by, listening expectantly. There was an odd expression of puzzlement upon his face. "But the old man was nowhere in sight. I followed the direction he'd been walking, and he wasn't anywhere. So, I went around to the back of the store. I even searched in the overgrown plot at the edge of the parking lot."

"Did you see him, Daddy?" asked Hoodoo with eyes wide.

"No, I didn't, and I spent a good deal of time looking—and regretting, too." Jack shook his head. "I'm very sorry that I didn't give that man my jacket as soon as I noticed him." Jack met each child's eyes. "It felt like a test to see if I would remember others while we're experiencing our own troubles. And I missed my chance to do something good for someone else."

There was silence for a moment before Nate said, "At least you were going to give it to him, Dad."

"That's not enough, son. I should have given it to him right away."

"You cared, and you looked all over for him," said Karen, bending to kiss her husband's forehead. Jack grabbed her hand and held it, pensive, as Karen sat down next to him.

"You've had a long day," she said. "Thank you for getting the money order. I'll mail it off. And supper's ready. Why don't you kids show your dad what we accomplished today while I dish everyone up?"

Vinca and Annie stretched out the garland, and Hoodoo—who had accomplished the least amount of its length—held it up in the middle, beaming. Nate stood by his dad's side, hands thrust into his pockets, not owning his contribution.

"Very nice," said Jack, and he smiled. He sighed and looked toward the ceiling, preoccupied with other thoughts, but then, looking at them again, he announced, "You know what? That garland needs a tree. Tomorrow afternoon we're going into the woods to find it."

"Yay!" Hoodoo dropped the garland as her sisters were attempting to coil it up and clapped her hands.

"Hoodoo, what the heck?" said Vinca. "And you don't have to be so loud!"

"Really, Dad?" said Nate. "No matter what?"

"Yes, son. I'm only working in the morning. You'll be helping me bring our tree home tomorrow afternoon."

The Woods

The kids were eating rice with milk and sugar when their dad stepped through the door, fresh flecks of purple paint adorning his trousers.

"Tree time!" he announced, smiling, as they jumped up from their seats at the table. "But finish eating first," he added.

Karen quickly made her husband a sandwich with grilled cheese. Her eagerness to bring home a tree rivaled that of her children.

The kids knew full well that they would have to champion for their favorite trees before their father's axe went to work, because their mom was extraordinarily picky about evergreens. After the tree was selected, another battle would wage, for their dad liked his trees pure, green like God made them. Their mom liked flocking, and if given the chance she sprayed can after can of fake snow onto the evergreen needles to inspire that "Idaho woodland" sort of feeling. Unfortunately, it also inspired coughing among the other members of the family as a thick, toxic cloud spread throughout the living room.

Bundled up, the Hoyles headed out excitedly. Jack grabbed his axe from the porch and took Karen's hand. Reuben trotted by his master's side, looking up expectantly. He barked twice to get Jack's attention, but when it became clear Jack had forgotten his righthand companion, Reuben nipped him on the hand to remind him.

"Whoa, Reuben!" exclaimed Jack, halting.

Reuben sat, staring up at Jack's face, his body tense, broad tail flicking. Man and dog faced each other. Finally, Jack held out the axe.

"Come," he commanded.

Reuben took the handle, his head dropping to one side with the sudden imbalance of weight. The kids watched as Reuben, resting the blade on the ground, maneuvered his teeth closer to the axe head. Once it was balanced in his mouth, he again trotted by his master's side, head held high.

The kids ran ahead, feet sinking into the muddy field, with Mandy prancing around them. Karen's arm was through Jack's, and they both smiled. The rent was paid, and it was beginning to feel like Christmas, even in a wet, drab world devoid of snow.

After following the line of trees away from the big hill, the family entered the woods by the path Jack and the kids had taken to get firewood a week before when the world had been white and astounding, an image now replaced by a muddy and muted landscape. They slowed their pace, spread out, and looked up into the cedar and other conifers to examine their splendor.

"This one's pretty."

"Look how green this one is!"

"Wow! Look at this big one!"

Though they heard one another calling out the details of various evergreens they encountered, muffled and yet echoed by the vast living woodland surrounding them, they took their own paths to find the perfect tree as they hiked through the forest.

Hoodoo meandered, gently touching the trees she passed, whispering words of greeting. She adored trees and thought them the best gift of nature to people; the woods were her favorite place in the whole world. There were times, though—especially in fall or winter—when they felt eerie and full of stealthy creatures, real or imaginary, that watched her.

The hardwood trees, even when winter-bare, invited human presence, sheltering and encouraging it like strong old friends. It was as if they were keenly aware of each guest within their domain, listening to them and laughing with them in the breeze that tickled their bare branches. To Hoodoo, each deciduous tree's personality was found in its individual shape.

The evergreens were scattered among the hardwoods, sharply contrasting, unchanged with the seasons, and intoxicating because of the rich smell they prescribed for the wintry woods in the absence of budding, blooming things. They were short and stout, tall and big. Some wore sweeping limbs while some were antisocial, growing tall but close, absorbed with themselves.

Jack was examining the runts, the scrawny ones, who had little hope, he felt, of growing into the tall and imposing evergreens that punctuated the Tennessee woods. He was tempted, as was his wont, to take one of these home, to give it the place of honor it was not likely to find amid the forest.

The only time he had gone by himself to choose their tree, in fact, he had brought back what the Hoyle children fondly remembered as their "Charlie Brown" tree. It had looked to be weeping; its branches drooped so much, and they were sparse and thinly woven. When Karen asked him why he had chosen it, he replied simply that he felt sorry for it.

As if sensing that her husband was going to repeat that mistake, Karen suddenly appeared at his elbow next to a tiny conifer that looked as if the snowfall of days before had sucked the last bit of life from it.

"Hello, honey. What are you looking at?"

Jack smiled back at her and asked, "Any luck finding that perfect tree?"

At that moment, Annie appeared, pointing to a small youthful tree not far away, "Can we get that one, too? For our bedroom?"

"No," responded Jack. He glanced at his wife while he continued, "We're here for a great big evergreen for all of us to enjoy in the living room. That one needs to be left alone to grow a few more years. And this one, too, I guess," he said doubtfully, studying the pitiful specimen before him one last time before turning away.

The family gathered again, each feeling disappointed in their search thus far, hoping to have better fortune together. Here and there throughout the woods, some evergreens had turned brown at the tip of their needles, like weary old men in the last winter of their existence, sad and brittle. Many other trees were scraggly, having been granted a place in the forest where they routinely starved for light. Some trees were grand but too tall for the house; others too short to inspire the necessary feeling.

They ventured deeper into the woods where the conifers began to thin out, occasionally catching the ghostly stirring of animals. They finally returned toward the field and were coming out of the woods by a different way when Karen halted with a gasp and pointed to a lonely tree at the edge of the forest, outlined vividly against a horizon of barren field and brown hills in the distance.

"That tree!" she said. "Why didn't we notice it before?"

"We're a good way from the path now," reminded Jack.

Karen approached it for a more thorough examination. Lushly green, broad and graceful, it looked like the smaller version of a Christmas tree one would find in some grand department store or exotic city center.

As she walked around it intently, she noticed its large sweeping branches had grown wild—not altogether even—but, oddly, that only enhanced its appeal.

She took Jack's cold, rough hand in her own, and he looked down at her as she continued to stare with bright eyes at the tree.

"You know what, honey?" she said, turning toward him. "This is the tree."

"I know," he laughed. "I could tell by your face when you first saw it. We might as well have an amazing tree this year. What do you think about this one, kiddos?" he asked, turning to look at their tilted faces.

Vinca nodded. "Momma is right. It is really pretty."

"I love it!" Hoodoo exclaimed. "It's so big."

Secretly, though, she felt a pang of sadness at the thought of this stately tree meeting her father's axe.

"Mom definitely found the perfect one," said Nate. He grinned. "Finally!"

"It doesn't have any brown spots, and it's not a Charlie Brown tree," Annie said.

"I think we've decided," said Jack, lowering the axe from his shoulder where it had rested in his hand when he took it from Reuben. "Now everyone stay back—I mean it, kids. And keep the dogs away, too."

Karen knelt by Reuben and encircled his broad neck with her arms. Annie corralled Mandy who panted at her side, watching the faces of the kids as she sensed that something exciting was about to happen.

Jack chopped off some of the lower branches to allow room to reach the trunk uninhibited. He walked around the tree, examining its shape, the ground, and the trees next to it.

"What are you doing, Dad?" Nate asked, impatient for the extraction of their Christmas tree to begin.

"I'm determining which way the tree should fall, son, so I know where to cut into the wood. You have to think these things through and take your time, so no one gets hurt." He paused and studied his son before asking, "Do you want to help me for the first little bit?"

"Sure!"

"I'm going to swing first," said Jack. "To get it started. Then you can take a couple of strokes. You're not going to hit the same spot every time, and that's alright—just in the general area. But you must obey me, okay?"

"Yes, sir!"

"Then watch."

Jack bent slightly as he swung the axe at an angle into the reddish-brown trunk. A wedge into the tree begun, he handed the axe to his son and guided his arms into a mock stroke a couple of times before he backed away to watch.

Nate's swings oscillated more than his dad's, but Jack let him wield the cumbersome tool four or five more times before he called out, "Okay, son!" He examined the slightly expanded wedge, and with a smile patted Nate's shoulder and added, "Good job!"

Jack swung the axe again and again, sweat beading on his face, as he worked at an awkward angle to fell the tree with his blade. Though the trunk was small considering the evergreen's size and compared to the hardwoods, it resisted him.

Hoodoo watched doubtfully and wondered if the tree didn't want to leave the woods, because she wouldn't want to, either.

"Be ready, all of you, and back up," said Jack at last, breathing hard and wiping his brow as the evergreen groaned and creaked. He landed one last stroke before dropping the axe and backing away, pushing his family farther behind him with outstretched arms.

The beautiful evergreen fell, its branches brushing a soft, final farewell against those of its neighbors. When it hit the ground, bouncing, the bottom of its trunk lifted into the air.

The family was silent for a moment, the dogs tense, and then Karen asked, "How are you going to carry it out?"

"Hold the trunk on my shoulder and drag it out," said Jack. "There's no better way, but I'll try to do the least amount of damage to the limbs."

He bent next to the stump, parallel to the fallen tree, and carefully hoisted its trunk onto his shoulder. Before rising he called, "Here, Reuben!"

The large black Lab came and took Jack's axe from his hand.

"Alright, everybody. Walk on ahead of me."

The procession of dogs, kids, parents, and tree crossed the field slowly as Jack leaned forward to leverage his weight into the task of hauling their Christmas bounty across the uneven cornfield. When they reached the front porch, Jack leaned the tree against one of two metal trellises there and rested with a gloved hand on his hip as the kids circled the tree, running their fingers along its needles.

"I'll help carry it in, Dad," said Nate, bending to lift some of its weight.

"Whoa! We need to trim it," said Jack. "After I take a few inches off the top, I want you to tell me which branches you want cut, honey," he said. "Just hold it up for me. You too, Vinca."

Jack cut a few inches off with a handheld clipper to make room for an angel. He took a couple of limbs from the bottom, so it would clear the floor. He stood back, brushing the hair from his face and wiping away more perspiration, as he looked at his wife expectantly.

She walked around it one more time but pronounced firmly after a few moments, "I don't think anything more needs to be cut away. It's beautiful the way it is."

"Good!" said Jack. "Let's get it into the house then."

"Wait!" cried Vinca. "I've got to lock Tommy in my room first, so he doesn't get outside."

She sped inside to tuck the tomcat safely into her room, for Tommy was possessed by a desire to be completely wild, she felt certain. Though he tolerated Vinca's affection more than anyone else's, he preferred to be left alone and would have been very content hunting alone in the woods for little creatures, never returning to the small, square house or the girl who loved him so much.

Karen stopped the screen door open with a rock when Vinca returned, and Annie held open the wooden door, flattening her body against the living room wall. Vinca and Hoodoo pushed the couch back.

Jack bounced the tree on the ground, but few if any needles fell from the freshly hewn evergreen.

He grabbed the trunk and Nate lifted the top, and with Nate following his father, they navigated the steps and pushed the grasping branches through the door. In the far corner opposite the kitchen, they leaned it against the wall where it disturbed a family of spiders that crawled down its trunk.

The tree was not what it should be, slumped in the corner.

"I'll have to go get the stand from the attic," said Jack.

"And the decorations," added Karen.

"And the decorations."

"Uh, Dad," said Nate, pointing. "Tommy and Sammy are using the tree as a scratching post."

"They can't hurt it. Don't worry."

But Nate felt that he had waited too long for their Christmas tree, so he grabbed Tommy and pulled him off while Sammy sat down and licked his dainty paws, watching. Tommy scratched Nate's arm, and Nate dropped him.

"Ouch!"

"Are we going to decorate the tree tonight?" asked Annie.

"I don't see why not," said Jack. "If we can find everything we need. Right now, however, I'm taking a coffee break."

With that, he heaved his tired body into his reliable chair.

Nails and Mistletoe

In the tiny hall of the Hoyle home, a yellow cord hung from the ceiling. With a tug Jack pulled on it, lowering the attic steps and folding them out into Nate and Hoodoo's room.

"Careful on these steps," he said to Nate, who came behind him as he climbed.

Hoodoo stepped up behind Nate, uninvited but intrigued by the excavation of the attic. As she started to scale the steep, narrow stairs after her brother, he turned, blocking the way with his arms.

"Who said you could come?" he asked, his chocolate brown eyes serious.

"But I just want to look. *Please.*"

"Let her come, Nate," their dad called out as he arrived at the top, feeling for another cord that would produce light from a single feeble bulb.

Nate pulled himself up behind Jack onto the dusty floor, and Hoodoo scampered close behind, brushing off her knees.

The attic was a graveyard for the discarded. Dust particles floated in the dim light over forgotten boxes of strange objects, traveling with the air disturbance produced by the slatted triangular window at the end of the house.

Attics, like basements, are curious places, and the Hoyle attic was no different. Every person who has lived in a house through its years leaves at least one box of sentimentally depreciated objects behind when they go. These boxes protruded from the shadows, listing on top of one another, and long neglected items peered out sullenly from the dark, rebuking the perpetrators of their fate. A scruffy teddy bear with stuffing poking out of its side held its glassy eyes fixedly on some darkened angle of the attic. It wasn't a bear that Hoodoo recognized. Its glazed stare and fractured seams made her sad.

She turned away from the abandoned bear, and her eye roved over a nearby box of old toys. She rummaged through it, heedless of poisonous spiders and other creepy-crawlies, until she pulled out a child's broom and mop set. Hoodoo held them up.

"Look, Daddy! It's my broom and mop set. Remember?"

She began to sweep the dirty attic, stooping because the set was too small for her, adding more ceaselessly floating particles to the air.

"Yes, I see," answered Jack, though he wasn't looking as he struggled to sort three or four large boxes by the accessway.

Hoodoo wandered farther into the dark and mysterious environs of the attic where it expanded over the living room.

"Stop!" said Nate, who also was exploring the forgotten and therefore interesting treasures of the attic.

"Why?" Hoodoo queried in alarm.

"Because if you step over there, you'll kill yourself," Nate replied in the matter-of-fact tone of a wise older brother. "The floor's too old and thin. You'll fall through it and die." He turned back to the excavation of a box.

Hoodoo backed away slowly, squinting into the dark to see how and where there was danger. She turned away from that realm of the attic that beckoned her to her doom and hurriedly went to stand by her dad, peering over his shoulder as he opened a box.

"Finally, another Christmas box," said Jack. "Come here, Nate."

Nate dumped a handful of seashells back into a container and reported to his dad's side.

"Do you think you can carry this down to your mother?" Jack asked. When Nate nodded, Jack said, "Be careful then."

Nate started down the rickety steps, shifting from side to side to see down them.

"Here, Hoodoo," said Jack as he held out a small red and green metal tree stand. "You can carry this down while I get the other box."

Hoodoo and Jack alighted at the bottom of the stairs where Karen stood waiting. Jack handed the box to her and folded the stairs back up into the attic. He pushed upward, and with a bang the rectangular inlet into the attic again sealed shut.

The sun angled toward the west, and Jack glanced out the big living room window at its decline.

"Let's get this tree into its stand," he said. "Honey, you hold the stand while I place the trunk in and tighten the screws, okay?"

Jack guided the heavy tree out from its corner and, grunting, slid it into the red and green stand.

"Hold it," he said to Karen and Vinca. They took the tree's weight from Jack's hands.

Jack pushed the trunk by degrees this way and that as he tightened the screws as much as he could into its thick diameter.

"Let go," he ordered, rising.

They stepped back. For one misleading moment, the lovely tree was upright. Then it fell backwards against the wall, tilting the stand off the floor.

"Let me fix that," said Jack.

"I think this side of the tree should face the room anyway," said Karen, pointing. "It's fuller."

Jack rotated the tree until the area Karen had indicated faced the living room. He twisted the screws again until they were secure.

"There. Let go."

This time the tree pitched forward. Mandy, who lay close by, scuttled out of the way with a yip. Jack and Karen caught it with their hands.

"Why won't it stay?" she asked.

"It's too heavy for this little stand."

He studied the situation, noting the holes at the end of each of the stand's three legs.

"I know what to do."

He disappeared into the kitchen, and they heard objects being thrust about in a drawer. Then he fetched something from behind the woodstove. When he turned, three long nails hung between his lips, and he gripped a hammer in his hand.

"Hold the tree up straight," he commanded through his teeth. "Help them, Annie."

Karen's eyes were wide as Jack stuck a nail into one of the holes at the end of the stand legs.

"Jack, honey—I don't know," she objected nervously. "Should we do that?"

Jack gave her a thumb's up before he put hammer to nail and drove it into the floor. The kids watched with curiosity as he did the same with the second and third nails.

When he finished, he stood and stepped back, daring the tree to fidget, to waver just the slightest bit from its position. It didn't move. It was vanquished.

"You put nails in the floor," said Hoodoo as if she had witnessed a magic trick.

"Yep. It shouldn't move now. We can decorate it soon."

"We get to decorate the tree! We get to decorate the tree!" Hoodoo sang, spinning around the living room with arms outstretched.

"Hoodoo, for crying out loud!" said Annie. "Why do you always have to be so loud?"

"Calm down, Hoodoo," her mother said.

Hoodoo gave her sister a sour look and sat down by the basement door, crossing her arms and deciding not to say anything ever again just to spite everyone else.

Jack drew Karen to him and placed an arm around her waist.

"What do you think of your tree?" he asked.

"It's lovely," she said. With a mischievous glint in her eye, she looked up at his face and added, "But it would be even better with flocking!"

"There's no money for that," replied Jack, as he kissed her forehead. He smiled. "Perhaps the only good thing about being low on funds."

He gazed at his wife for a moment before adding, "Nate and I are going to get mistletoe for an extra festive touch."

"There's not much daylight left," said Karen, glancing out the window and following him as he headed toward their room. "You might get hurt."

Jack reemerged with his lineman boots from the powerline days. The long, thick safety belt he once used for wrapping around powerline poles was slung over his shoulder, but the climbing hooks that worked with it remained in his bedroom closet. These relics from the powerline reminded Jack of the risky work of his younger days when, as he often told his children, he became a man.

The boots were difficult to pull on. Absent from his feet for some time, they seemed to have shrunk. When he succeeded after several tugs in wrestling them on, he laced up their long, thick laces.

Karen watched him, clasping and unclasping her hands.

"Please be careful."

"I always am. Come on, son."

Hoodoo jumped up.

"Can I come, too?"

"Hoodoo, stay here with me, and we'll sort the decorations," said Karen.

Hoodoo looked pleadingly at her dad.

"Stay with your mom," said Jack, resting his hand on her head as she looked up at him. "Nate and I will be back soon, and then you can help me figure out where to hang the mistletoe, okay?"

"Alright."

Jack patted her head and hurried out the door with his work gloves. Nate followed, cold air rushing in as he slammed the door behind him.

While they were absent the girls watched parts of *Babes in Toyland* on the small black-and-white TV, one of Karen's favorite holiday movies, as they looked over the baubles in the boxes from the attic. Hoodoo was excited to see and touch the old decorations again, but she looked out the window repeatedly, wanting to glimpse her dad and hoping to decorate the tree soon.

Jack led Nate quickly down the lane, and the boy struggled to match his father's strides.

"Where do we find the mistletoe, Dad?" Nate asked his father's back as they walked briskly.

"I saw a large cluster in one of those oak trees at the edge of the lane right by the creek," said Jack. He looked over at the horizon. "But we have to hurry if we want to retrieve it."

Jack slowed and began examining the trees on his left.

"Aha!" He gestured for his son to come closer. Putting an arm around Nate's shoulder, he pointed up. "See that? Way up there? That's mistletoe."

"Am I going to climb and get it?"

"No, son. I'll do the climbing."

Jack hoisted himself up onto the lowest branch, the belt latched loosely around his waist, and climbed through the oak's large branches in the failing light. When he reached the green but frail-looking mistletoe, he hugged the wide tree alternately with each arm while latching the belt on his waist around its trunk until it was secure.

Nate sucked in his breath as he watched, anxious for his dad's safety. The feathery white and green mistletoe did not seem worth the trouble to him. Nevertheless, he felt pride that, as his dad's only son, he was called out as backup on dangerous missions like these. And he watched for the first sprigs of mistletoe to drop from his dad's hands toward the lane.

The sun sank that late afternoon as if discouraged by the lack of color in the world. With no ribbons of pink, coral, or indigo in the winter sky to bid it farewell, it was an insignificant white light on the edge of the world for one brave moment before it left speedily to awaken a sleeping hemisphere.

As it dropped below the horizon, Karen came to the window. Within moments, she saw Nate and Jack turning the corner into the driveway below the walnut tree.

"Oh, thank goodness!" said Karen, going to the door.

She opened it as Jack laid his hand upon the knob, and the two guys blew in with bunches of leafy, thin green plants in their hands punctuated by small ivory-white berries. The ends of their noses were red with cold, and their cheeks flushed with yuletide activity. The smell of Mother Earth, of pebbles and dust on the lane, of damp, decaying leaves, and of rich, dark, living soil beneath the trees, accompanied them into the warm house. Immediately, they hurried to the old woodburning stove to warm themselves.

Jack turned to face his wife and daughters, still rubbing his hands, and asked, "Now where should we hang this mistletoe? Hoodoo?"

Hoodoo smiled at her dad for remembering his promise, but then her face grew serious as she looked around the living room.

"The front door?"

"Seems like a good place," replied Jack.

"The kitchen doorway, too—so you and mom can kiss," added Annie, giggling.

"Always a good idea," responded Jack with a wink at Karen.

He picked up his hammer and gathered more nails from various places and began to secure bunches of mistletoe above the front door. He hung a few sprigs from a nail over the doorway of the kitchen. Nate followed his dad around with the clusters in his hand. With the leftover sprigs Jack lined the windowsills of their home and put the last bunch on the living room shelf.

He examined the room when he was done and said, "Doesn't that look cheery? It's beginning to feel a lot like Christmas in here."

He caught Karen in a tight embrace as she came to stand beside him in the kitchen doorway.

"A kiss," he said, pointing to the delicate sprig above. "We're under the mistletoe, after all."

Karen laughed, her face as flushed as it had been when they all sledded down the big hill. She wrapped her arms around his neck and gave him a long kiss while their children grimaced at each other and rolled their eyes.

Christmas Tapestry

Cozy warmth emanated from the woodstove. Christmas songs played softly on the radio.

Supper had been a simple affair—noodles in beef broth with boiled potatoes on the side—but it didn't matter to the kids. They knelt and rummaged through the decoration boxes, each plucking out special ornaments that they claimed as their own. Some they had made in school for their parents; others were given to them by friends; and there were those with mysterious origins and stories that appealed to their different personalities.

The kids had also inherited simple but cherished ornaments made of felt from a relative left behind in Idaho. Vinca's was a rocking horse; Annie's a teddy bear; Nate's a Santa Claus; and Hoodoo's was, of course, a snowman.

Additionally, Vinca possessed several that her capable hands had made of cloth and wire for her family, and many that had been given to her by her friends.

A large plastic unicorn was Annie's favorite ornament. It shimmered with glitter, and the light shone through it like stained glass. Because Annie had taken ballet lessons as a small girl and had the

96

slender build of one, several ballerinas were also in her collection.

Nate loved Santa Claus and claimed all the miniature ones that found their leisure hanging on a tree. He also had a wooden candle, but his prized ornament was of a plastic boy in a multi-colored baseball uniform with a bat and glove in his hands.

All the snowmen belonged to Hoodoo, along with two glittery toy soldiers she had constructed of clothespins at school.

The kids made four piles on the floor in preparation to adorn the tree.

"No, kids. Put them back," said Karen who was sitting with her feet curled beneath her on the couch. "Your dad has to put the lights on first."

"Oh, right," said Annie, gingerly returning the unicorn to its box.

"That's right," said Nate, but he kept his pile of St. Nicks separate.

Hoodoo heaved a sigh. She cradled the felt snowman in her hand as she sat down by her mother.

Karen laughed and took her hand.

"Be patient," she said.

In a low voice Jack sang along with a carol on the radio, filled with Christmas cheer as he brought out four strings of lights in a mass together, two colored sets and two clear sets, to untangle them.

"That's right, kids. Lights first," he said with a smile.

That smile began to look like an unnatural fixture glued to his face as he wrestled with the lights. Soon, the smile abandoned him altogether, and, instead of cheerfully singing, he muttered under his breath.

The kids watched the age-old battle with the tangled lights, interest mingling with impatience. Karen held a hand to her mouth. The corners of her mouth crept up, and her body quivered with suppressed laughter as she watched her husband.

"Ah!" exclaimed Jack, as he held up one colored string like a snake in the wilderness, denouncing all previous frustration in a moment of glory, and advanced with it to the nearest outlet to test it out. Perhaps because of its age, it chose not to light up as expected.

"Now what's the problem!"

"Maybe the bulbs aren't screwed in tight," said Karen.

"It probably won't work at all. *Stupid thing*," said Jack, but he checked each bulb's tightness in the socket. After a few minutes of this repetition, he twisted one miscreant bulb, and the entire row of lights lit up against the wood floor. Jack's smile returned.

"Hooray!" said Hoodoo.

"Yes—good!" agreed her father, implying that consequences for this set of lights would have been severe if they had not chosen to light at that moment. Each strand he tested in turn, and, with surprise and gratification, the family watched each illuminate. Jack took the first set to the tree.

"The colors are so rich on that one, honey," said Karen. "It was always my favorite. Where did we get it? Do you remember?"

"It was the Christmas we spent in Nebraska, I think," he answered.

Beginning at the top, Jack wound the lights between and around the elegant conifer's branches. That strand finished, he grabbed another colored strand and coiled it around the lower branches. Then he began anew at the top with a set of clear lights followed by the last until the tree was woven with four strings of lights.

"We need an extension cord," said Jack.

Again, the family heard odds and ends thrust about in the kitchen drawer. Jack came out with a brown extension cord.

"Who gets to put the angel on the tree?" Nate asked.

"Who did it last year?" Karen asked Jack as he unwound the extension cord.

He paused a moment and then said, "Vinca, I think."

"Then, it's Annie's turn," said Karen to Nate. She added as she smoothed his thick, unruly locks gently with her hand, "And it'll be your turn next year."

Jack angled his body behind the big tree and plugged the lights into the cord.

When he reemerged from behind the tree's prickly branches, Karen shut off the living room light.

A hush descended on the family as the lights shimmered from the tree, waking upon the ceiling in a radiant, multi-hued halo and filtering through the winter darkness of the room to imbue it with a warm glow.

"Make them blink, Daddy," said Hoodoo.

"The colored ones?"

"Yeah!"

"I'll see if I have the right bulbs."

Flipping the light switch on again, Jack searched through the box and discovered a tiny bag with extra lights, unscrewed the first bulb in the topmost set, and put on what he hoped was a blinker. After some doubtful seconds, the string of lights flashed. He did the same with the second strand of colored lights.

"That's even better," he said, stepping back.

Hoodoo ran to turn off the lights once more, and then she stared at their Christmas tree as colors flashed from its graceful, sweeping limbs onto the ceiling and walls, a bleeding spectrum of brilliant light, while the white lights shone steadily and gracefully against the evergreen.

"Adeste Fideles" came softly from the stereo, and the mood in the room was like a rich Christmas tapestry hanging in the Hoyle home, deeply red like the tint of wine with a dark green tree threaded subtly into the fabric.

"Turn up the radio please, Vinca," said Jack, and his eye fell on the popcorn garland. "Baby, do you want to put this up yourself?" he asked, picking it up.

"May I?" She looked around.

"Go ahead, Mom," said Annie, smiling, as she turned back on the living room light.

"Not too close to the lights," added Jack.

Karen took one end of the garland from his hands, and as he supported the rest of it, she began at the top and gingerly coiled it around the tree, stepping back occasionally to examine her progress and to adjust the loops of the garland.

"There," she said when she was satisfied.

Hoodoo clapped her hands.

"We made that," she told her dad again.

"I know you did. And now it's time for you kids to decorate our tree." As they scrambled to the box, jostling each other out of the way, he added, "No rushing! We need to hang up the Christmas balls first, remember? Come here, and line up, oldest to youngest."

There was more shoving and jockeying for position, but they managed at last to present an even line, by age, before their father.

Jack picked up a shiny blue sphere, placing a wire hanger through its metallic top.

"Blue for my firstborn child," he said, smiling as he held it out to Vinca.

"Thanks, Daddy."

Vinca studied the tree to find the perfect branch for the first ornament.

Jack held up a golden Christmas ball, placing a hanger through it as well. Annie stood near him, waiting.

He extended it to her. "Gold for my golden-haired girl."

Annie took it and found a spot for it that she deemed right.

The next ornament was bright red in color, and Nate opened one hand to receive it as he slung an arm over his dad's shoulder. Jack placed it in

Nate's palm and said, "Red, for my son who will carry on my bloodline."

Hoodoo gave her dad a slobbery kiss on the cheek. She stepped back and waited for him to speak.

"And green is for my little nature girl," he ended, holding up the forest green sphere by its little tree hook. As she ventured to find its place among the others, Jack concluded, "Go to it, now, kids—get all those ornaments up."

"Don't leave any bare spots," said Karen.

Jack sat back, smiled at his wife, and reached for her hand.

Vinca held up a petite and flimsy angel, her body comprised of cardboard and her face made of plastic. She had short blond curls, a pink dress, and a tiny hymnal in her hands.

"Here's the angel, Mom."

"Annie will put that up the very last thing."

From their comfortable, warm spot on the couch, Jack and Karen watched their children adorn the family tree. When they saw hesitation, they gave advice, pointing out places that were sparse. Now and then, Karen leaned forward, willing her four kids to distribute the remaining ornaments evenly and glancing at Jack often, sharing her exasperation with a look that elicited a grin from him in reply.

Annie finished with her portion first, while the ever-efficient Nate was a close second, but, of course, those two had been racing all along.

"Here, Hoodoo," said Vinca when she saw her littlest sister had nothing left to hang and was disappointed. "You can help me hang the rest of mine."

It was a generous offer, for big sister Vinca shared her mother's sensibilities about a balanced tree, even stealthily moving her siblings' ornaments a degree or two.

When the oldest and youngest had finished decorating, the kids sat by their dad on the couch while their mom walked around the tree, studying it.

"Well done, kids," she said, refraining from rearranging their handiwork. "We certainly have lots of ornaments we've collected over the years."

"Are you ready to place the angel now?" Jack asked Annie, getting up. She nodded. "Okay," he said, "come on. I'll help you."

The frail angel in her hand, he hoisted her up in his arms.

"Can you reach?" he asked, straining to keep her gangly frame steady.

"I think I can, Dad."

She held the singing angel aloft and placed it over the blunt end of the topmost limb. The angel's diaphanous wings dusted the ceiling.

Jack put Annie down and gave her a hug.

"Our little angel," said Karen as she glanced up into the ancient ornament's sweet face. "She's a little worn, but I will never want a different one."

"We bought that the year you were born," she added to Vinca, "because she looked like you. Like you and Annie, too. You both used to have the blondest hair when you were babies."

Jack rearranged the top set of lights, so that one orb, a blue one, flashed on and off through the angel.

"It's only missing one thing," said Nate.

"What's that, son?"

"Candy canes."

"Maybe I can pick some up on the way home from work tomorrow. That shouldn't cost too much."

The family studied the final effect of the tree as it stood in its appointed corner. It truly was big, made larger by the myriad ornaments it easily supported and by the reflection it cast against the night-darkened and opaque panes of the windows nearest it.

Glancing at the windows, Jack was reminded of the hour.

"Time for bed, kids."

No More Painting

Before Jack got paid on Monday, he waited on the owner to examine every corner, line, and crevice of her formal dining room in a house full of large and expensively furnished rooms.

When at last she handed him the check, it was for a few dollars more than he expected.

He must have raised his eyebrows for she explained demurely in her genteel southern accent, "I gave you a fifteen-dollar tip. For Christmas."

Jack studied the tiny, well-dressed woman before him with her thin eyebrows and perfectly coiffed hair over a face fuller than seemed natural for her size or age. Fifteen dollars was little to her, and it would not rescue his family's Christmas.

Still, it was more than he had expected.

He smiled and nodded. "Thank you, ma'am. That was kind of you."

The extra fifteen dollars would pay for candy canes and some groceries.

And perhaps she would tell her friends and family about the man who painted her fabulous purple dining room as they enjoyed ham and prime rib on Christmas Day, and he would get more work. Though he dreaded the thought of returning to painting for a living, he meant to do whatever necessary to provide for his family.

After stopping by the convenience store to cash the check, lamenting the fee they withdrew from his pay to do so, Jack went to the grocery store on his way home to buy those candy canes his son had missed on their beautiful tree the night before.

He also acquired milk, a dozen eggs, bread, margarine, sugar, and flour. For a long time, he stood and looked at the hams, debating whether they could afford it with work so uncertain and funds so low. In the end he walked away with a package of ground beef, deciding that his family would have ham once he knew where his next paycheck would come from, even if it was not eaten on Christmas Day.

As he exited the store and was placing the groceries in his trunk, Jack noticed a young man with his family nearby. The man, short and wiry, was leaning beneath the hood of a small car. His wife stood by him, a worried expression on her face as she watched him examine the automobile, and two young children ran around the car as it sat in the parking lot.

Jack shut the trunk and approached.

"Good afternoon," he said. "I'm afraid I don't know anything about cars, but is there some way I can help you folks?"

The wife, a petite woman in baggy clothes with deep brown hair knotted clumsily at the back of her head, watched Jack warily. The young man pushed thin, sandy-colored hair back from his high forehead and stood up, facing Jack, looking him over for just a moment with deep grey eyes.

"We need to get into Nashville," he answered finally. "My wife has family there. I know what's wrong with the car. We just don't have money to fix it. We just need to get to Nashville," he reiterated, glancing at his two children, a little girl and an older boy. The two of them had stopped playing to listen to this conversation, hovering near their mother.

"I'm not a mechanic, and I don't have much," Jack told them, reaching into his back pocket for his wallet. He flipped it open and saw a twenty-dollar bill at the front of the thin fold of cash. He hesitated for just a moment, and then pulled it out, extending it toward the man. The husband and wife looked at each other, and with widened eyes, the woman nodded sharply to her husband. When he came forward and accepted it from Jack's hand, Jack said, "I give it to you in Jesus's name. Hope it helps."

The man nodded awkwardly, unsure of how to respond to this odd and unexpected declaration, but he said softly, "Thank you. This will help."

"Is there anything else I can do?" asked Jack. He added hastily, "Give me a minute."

From the trunk of his car, he pulled out one of the boxes of candy canes. Coming back over, he handed it to the woman.

"I thought your kids might like those."

"Thank you," she said and smiled, displaying crooked teeth, but her thin face and dark, worried eyes softened.

"Merry Christmas," said Jack, and he turned back to his car.

"Merry Christmas!" the little girl called out, bouncing by her mother's side, anxious for a candy cane.

Jack said an earnest prayer that the young family would find their way to Nashville as he drove home, but even as he did so, he thought of the twenty dollars that his own family needed. To assuage his worry, he reminded himself that his client had paid him more than expected, so he was only short five dollars. Regardless, he knew he was right to help, as he recalled the old man without a coat from a few days before.

These thoughts faded when he came to the end of his lane and saw Barry Barton's truck parked by the mailbox. What could his friend want, he wondered, so close to Christmas?

Karen heard Jack pull into the drive and was relieved, for though she could sometimes engage Barry in conversation, he had been sitting in her home for more than a half-hour, looking, if not unhappy, not altogether comfortable, either, and the kids stared at him as if he were a curiosity despite Karen's repeated efforts to get her children to concentrate on something else.

In various ways, Hoodoo especially had tried to get his attention, fascinated by any friend of her dad's, but Barry's face, overgrown by his great gray beard, had remained impassive as he stiffly stared back at the kids but uttered barely a word to them.

Karen knew Barry liked her and respected that she chose to work in the woods with her husband, but even her questions about his family had been answered in low tones and with few words.

Barry stood eagerly and smiled for the first time when Jack opened the door.

"Hey, Barry! How are you?" Jack asked as the two men shook hands.

"Hey, Jack. Christmas shoppin'?"

"No, I was painting a house, and then I dropped by the store for groceries. Kids, go get them from the car," he added to his children. He faced his friend again. "How have you been? Are things improving at all?"

Jack couldn't keep the note of hope from his voice.

"Well, yeah, I came abou' that," said Barry. "I know ya'll been worryin', and I sure hate to lose ya and Karen to 'nother buyer."

"We don't sell to anyone else, Barry," Jack replied, and then he waited with bated breath.

But Barry said, "Do ya mind if we go outside? Bit warm in here."

Jack and Karen glanced at each other before Jack answered, "No problem, Barry."

The two men went outside, and Barry leaned against the door of his truck, looking relaxed as he gazed across the field behind the Hoyle home.

"Good woods ya'll got there," he said to Jack.

"Yep," said Jack. "We enjoy them."

There was a pause, and then Barry studied Jack's face and enunciated in his slow drawl, "I managed to get one o' my customers back from Adam Riggs, Jack. One o' my good customers."

Jack's heart pounded, and he felt the weight that had been on his shoulders for the past several days lift. Yet it still hovered above him, ready to crash back down.

"I called this woman up and presented my case, so to speak," Barry went on. "And she said she wasn't much int'rested in giving Riggs her business when she's worked with me fer so long—even if he did sell a bit cheaper. She bought up some of my inventory—at a slight discount, ya know—and said she'd talk to 'nother big customer fer me, too, a friend of hers. So, I'm gonna start buyin' wreaths again."

"Barry, that's good news! Will she buy all winter?"

"Yeah, until the spring."

"Oh, man," Jack said. "That is really great news. *Really great news.*"

Barry's melancholy brown eyes gazed kindly into his friend's face, and then he yanked open the door of his truck and pulled something out of the glovebox.

"Ya want a cigar?"

"No. But thank you."

Barry lit a cigar and then drew on it for a few moments before asking, "Yer kids excited about Christmas? They were showing me yer tree, the one ya'll got from the woods. Real pretty."

"It will be tight this year," Jack answered frankly. "But they're good kids, and they enjoyed getting the tree and decorating it."

"I can't tell ya how sorry I am abou' things," said Barry, looking down as he drove some cigar ash into the dirt with his boot. "I wouldn' have put ya in a bind for the world."

"It was only for a few days," said Jack, "and we managed. Besides, it wasn't your fault. That's business, and then the snow hurt us, too. It's just the way things go sometimes."

"Well, work'll be better now," said Barry. Then he chuckled, "I was gonna be in a bad way if it didn't shape up righ'. I figure I woulda had to do somethin' else—at least til ginseng season came along. Trouble is, I only like workin' in the woods."

Jack laughed in agreement. His friend even smelled like the Tennessee woods—the woods and Swisher Sweet cigars. "I know what you mean," he said. "I just got done painting a lady's house—you would hate being stuck indoors for days like that—and I disliked every minute of it. But I would keep doing it to support my family. Luckily, and thanks to you, I get to go back to the woods, too."

They stood in companionable silence for a while, the smoke from Barry's cigar floating on the chill breeze.

"So I can sell to you the day after Christmas?" asked Jack.

"Hey, I'll buy some righ' now if ya got any," Barry answered.

Jack laughed. "No, I don't. But I will."

"Hey; ya want a candy cane?" asked Barry suddenly, again reaching into his truck.

Even though there was a whole box of them inside the house, Jack didn't want to say no after declining the cigar.

"Sure."

"Here's some for yer kids, too," said Barry, dropping several into Jack's hand.

What goes around does indeed come around, thought Jack, recalling the family in the grocery store parking lot.

"Thanks," he told Barry. "They'll appreciate it."

"They'll look good on that tree they're so proud o'," said Barry with a grin. "Pep'mint and sugar make everythin' better."

Annie came down the front porch steps with two mugs of cocoa in her hands.

"Homemade," she announced proudly as she handed one to each of them.

"Here, Annie," said Jack. "Take in these candy canes to your brother and sisters."

"Thanks, Daddy."

"Don't thank me. Thank Mr. Barton. He gave them to me."

"Thank you, Mr. Barton."

Barry nodded awkwardly and looked out to the woods.

"Bye, it's cold out here," said Annie, turning back to the house.

"Tell your mom we said thanks," called Jack after her.

For an hour or more, as Jack swirled one of the peppermint canes through his cocoa cup, Barry talked to Jack in his leisurely manner. Jack felt so grateful and so lighthearted that he listened to his friend without any attempt to hurry him on.

"What time is it, ya know?" Barry finally asked.

"Sorry, I don't have a watch."

"That's a'right. I keep an old 'un on the dash." He rummaged through the layer of junk that lined his dashboard.

"Whoa, it's righ' on five o'clock," said Barry, a hint of alarm in his tone. "I guess we been talking fer some time. Was s'posed to take my oldest to choir practice. I best be headin' home."

Jack smiled broadly as he shook his friend's hand. "I'm glad you came by. I can't tell you how much we appreciate this news."

"Maybe we could do somethin' for New Year's Eve, Jack. A kinda potluck. I know where to get some homemade mulberry wine. Strong stuff but real good, help us celebrate still having work after Christmas. No more paintin', right?"

"No more painting," Jack replied.

Barry got in his truck and started the engine.

"Come see me when ya got some wreaths. I'll buy as many as ya'll roll."

"Sure thing."

"Merry Christmas, Jack."

"Merry Christmas, Barry."

Train Tracks

Karen was making sugar cookies in the kitchen with the staples Jack had brought home from the store. After she rolled out the dough, the kids cut it with metal cookie cutters and placed the shapes on a cookie sheet that was charred from years of baking sweets and savories.

When Jack came into the kitchen, his wife looked at him expectantly, the question already in her eyes if not yet on her lips.

He grinned at her as she came towards him.

"Can he... is he...?"

"Yes," answered Jack. "Barry is able to buy our wreaths again."

"God bless him!"

"Yes," Jack agreed, "God bless him."

She quickly put the cookies in the oven, and then turned to face her husband again.

"If only this news had come a bit sooner, we might have been able to buy something special for Christmas dinner."

"That can't be helped," responded Jack. "The money in my wallet is all the money we have in the world, and it's less than thirty dollars. We still need to be careful until we can get paid again, and more bills are coming in January."

"So we can't have a ham?" asked Nate.

"I don't think so, son. I really wanted to get one, but I just don't think we can afford it right now. Maybe we'll have one for New Year's."

All the children had been listening to this exchange intently, trying to decipher the chance of presents, even small ones, but their faces fell at this pronouncement.

Jack tried not to notice their expressions, and he hastily changed the subject.

"Those cookies will taste good with this cocoa. Did you kids eat your candy canes already?"

Nate and Hoodoo nodded their heads.

"Ours are on the tree," said Vinca, indicating Annie.

"You got a whole other box, didn't you, Dad?" asked Nate.

"Yes, I did."

"Can we hang them up now?"

"Sure."

When the kids left the kitchen, Jack said to Karen, "I'm going to go into the woods and down the lane to try and get grapevine tomorrow, to start rolling."

"We'll both work tomorrow."

Jack's face was earnest as he placed a hand on his wife's arm as she was cutting out more cookies. She looked up into those pale green eyes, now sad, that she loved.

"If you could just figure out something special to make for dinner tomorrow, maybe with that ground beef...."

Karen nodded, her throat suddenly tight.

"I'll make the best dinner I possibly can," she promised.

As the family ate supper that evening and watched the lights blinking on the tree a few feet away from them at the end of the table, Nate asked, "What were your Christmases like when you were a little boy, Dad?"

"Uh, well..." Jack put a fist to his chin as he sat back, thinking. "Well, they were a lot like ours. Simple. My parents never had a lot of money. You remember I told you we moved around a lot? Well, your grandpa used to preach revivals and take little churches here and there. Most of the time we were in small towns in Idaho. But one year we were in Phoenix, I remember. We all got oranges in our stockings, a big treat for us kids at that time. They have citrus trees all around there. And hundreds of oranges litter the ground by the roadways."

"Yeah, but do you remember any presents that you got? I mean that you really, really liked?"

Jack thought for a minute and then leaned forward, putting his elbows on the table.

"We didn't get many big gifts, Nate. Let me see..." Jack rubbed his beard as he looked down at his plate and tried to recall. "Actually... yes, there was a Christmas when I got something I had always wanted." He looked up at his son. "But not from my parents."

The kids leaned toward him in anticipation, waiting.

"We had just moved to a new town a couple of months before, I think," began Jack. "I can't remember the name of it now, but the people in the church knew that our family didn't have much. It doesn't usually pay well to be a preacher, especially if you have five children to support. Anyway, the church families got together and collected a bunch of toys for us. They weren't new—these people didn't have much money, either—but just toys that their kids no longer wanted or played with."

"When they delivered the big box to us one evening, my parents let us take turns going through it. I had to wait for my big brothers to decide what they wanted before I got the chance to look, and I was afraid there wouldn't be anything good left. When it was finally my turn, I looked in that box and spied pieces of something I had always hoped for."

The children listened intently, inching their chairs closer to their father's during pauses. They loved Jack's stories, whether true ones or those he made up while working in the woods.

"What was it, Daddy?" asked Vinca.

"It was an electric train engine and some tracks. The train engine was red and silver and had Santa Fe printed on it. There was a caboose, too. The only problem was the track. There were no curved pieces—they were all straight. But there were several of them. So I set up my train in the basement of the church, where they used to have Sunday school, and I pushed my Santa Fe engine back and forth on that straight line of track." Jack demonstrated with his right hand. "And I imagined all the great places I would go when I got older. I spent a lot of time pushing that train back and forth."

Jack looked up then and was surprised by his children's faces.

"What about the controller for the train?" asked Nate, almost angrily.

"There wasn't one, son."

Karen watched the kids anxiously. All of them were looking at their dad mournfully, and the girls' eyes were misty.

"What's wrong?" asked Jack, confused by their reactions. "I loved my train set."

"But all you had were the straight pieces!" wailed Hoodoo.

She and her siblings pictured their dad as a pitiful little boy, all alone in a church basement, pushing an electric train back and forth on a line of track that led to nowhere.

"This story wasn't supposed to make you cry," said Jack desperately, looking at his daughters' teary eyes. "I really did like my train set. It didn't matter to me that it didn't have all its parts. I used my imagination. Like you kids do when you build fairy houses by the creek or army men forts."

"Someday, Daddy," vowed Vinca, "when we're all grown up... we're going to pitch in and buy you a real train set."

"Yeah," said Annie.

Jack stood up and pushed back his chair.

"You all need to cheer up," he admonished, "instead of thinking about my old train set."

"It wasn't a set," Nate muttered.

"But I liked it just fine, anyway," Jack told him, as he took his plate into the kitchen.

When he came back out to stand by the woodstove, Nate approached his dad and said solemnly, "Thank you for getting me my train set, Dad."

"You're welcome."

Jack gave his son a hug. Nate held onto his father for longer than usual, and Jack observed the glum looks that plagued the rest of the family.

"I lost my desire for a train set a long time ago," he announced. "But I haven't lost my desire for my own kids to have a good Christmas. Let's make a list," continued Jack, "of all the things we wanted to have this year—food, presents, anything. Then maybe when work gets better for your mom and me, we might be able to get them. It won't be Christmas anymore, but we can still have a celebration."

Vinca got up and went into her bedroom. When she came back, she handed her dad a sheet of paper and a pen.

"Thank you, Vinca." Jack grabbed a book to write on. "Okay, we're going from youngest to oldest." He wrote something at the top of the paper before looking up at his littlest girl. "So, Hoodoo, tell me what you'd like to have for Christmas. The thing you want most."

"I know what I want, Daddy. I want a Barbie doll."

Placing the paper on top of the book, Jack wrote Hoodoo's request down in bold letters.

"How about you, Nate? Or were you satisfied with candy canes?" Jack asked with a smile.

"I want a G.I. Joe, Dad."

"Alright. And what do you want, Annie?"

"I want some art supplies," she answered. "And a new shirt or something, please."

Jack added these to the list. He hoped to get her new clothes, and he understood her desire for art supplies. His second daughter took after him; Jack had drawn and painted regularly once.

He turned to Vinca.

"What I really want more than anything else?" she asked.

Jack nodded. "What you really want more than anything else."

"Well, I'd like some new clothes, too. And books. But what I really, really want right now are cordial cherries. Chocolate cherries. Remember, Daddy, when you'd buy them every year? It doesn't seem like Christmas without them."

"I wouldn't mind some myself," said Jack as he added it to the list. He looked up at his wife. "And now it's up to you, honey."

"If I had to choose just one thing," she said, "it would be a Christmas ham."

"Yeah!" Nate applauded. "A ham!"

"That just leaves you," said Karen to her husband. "What do you want?"

Jack smiled at her fondly.

"I just want some of your homemade apple pies."

"Pies," repeated Hoodoo wistfully.

Jack added apples to the Christmas list. Then he collected some tacks from the living room shelf. He tacked their list against the basement door to the left of the woodstove.

The rest of the family gathered around. In large letters at the top, it stated boldly, "The Hoyle Family Christmas List."

They were all silent for a while, reading the items on their list.

Hoodoo looked up at her father.

"Maybe God will see it and send Santa to bring them to us."

Jack reached down and smoothed her long, dark hair.

"God has more important things to do than worry about our Christmas list, Hoodoo. But it's a nice thought."

Mr. Johnson

Christmas Eve came like a mischievous child. The day was sunny and warmer than preceding days. The weather defied the legend of Christmas snow, but it wasn't an uncommon December day in Tennessee.

The Hoyle family ate scrambled eggs for breakfast, and soon after Nate and Hoodoo began begging their mother for the sugar cookies made the day before.

Jack was in a good mood as he left the house to gather grapevine from the woods and lane. He found more than expected; it had been a while since he and Karen had gleaned the wild vine from their own surroundings.

Hauling large rolls of it back to the house was hard work, but he wanted to remain near his family. As he worked, the children gazed out at him periodically from the front window. Hoodoo and Nate came to sit on the concrete porch for a while, watching and talking to him, but though the day was comparatively mild for winter, the cold porch soon chased them back inside to devise other pastimes.

For hours Jack concentrated cheerfully on his work, picking up the vines, rolling them deftly into pretty wreaths that others would see in a craft or florist shop, admire, and purchase without ever imagining the working man who had fashioned them with his hands for a living. Though he planned to work late on Christmas Eve, shaping and clipping the vine with the clippers in his back pocket, he was peaceful. There would be money for groceries and bills after Christmas.

Four o'clock came and went, and Jack was sweating in his shirt and gloves even as the sun began its decline toward the hills in the west, when he heard a car coming down the road. The sound grew nearer until he spied an unfamiliar vehicle approaching between the barren trees that lined the lane.

Jack stopped rolling, anxiously wondering who it could be, and waited for it to pull up.

A large white van turned the final corner by the mailbox and pulled up behind Jack's car in the drive underneath the walnut tree. Reuben barked gutturally at the unknown automobile, while Jack approached, impatient to learn a stranger's reason for disturbing his family on Christmas Eve.

When the driver's side door opened, a tall, lanky man wearing a cowboy hat stepped out, with a clipboard in his hand.

Jack kept an uneasy eye on Reuben. For a Labrador, the dog was fiercely protective and often intimidated strangers with his unusually large size.

But the man didn't act as if the dog was a threat, and Reuben made no move to molest him, though he watched the man's movements carefully.

The stranger smiled at Jack. His brown eyes were pale, almost amber, contrasting with the dark, nearly black hair beneath his hat.

"Can I help you?" asked Jack, still holding an unfinished wreath in his hand.

"Are you Jack Hoyle?" the man inquired in a pleasant baritone.

"Yes, I am," replied Jack, surprised.

"I'm Chris Johnson, Mr. Hoyle. I work with a local organization, and your name was given to us for our Christmas list this year. I have a delivery for you in the back of my van."

"For me?"

"Yes, sir. Some Christmas boxes for you and your family."

Jack tossed his wreath aside and followed the tall man to the back of the van. The man opened the double back doors, and Jack saw three large boxes there.

"Which one is mine?" asked Jack.

"All of them."

"All of them?"

"Yes, sir."

"I don't understand," said Jack. "Who gave you our name?"

"I couldn't tell you, Mr. Hoyle. All I know is your name was on my list for delivery. And those three boxes are yours."

"I must be the very last one on your route, I guess," said Jack.

"To be honest, you are. I almost didn't make it out this way, but I felt like I should."

"Well, thank you," Jack replied hesitantly.

Mr. Johnson handed out one of the boxes to Jack. It was heavy.

"I'll just bring these others in for you," he said, and he slid them out, one on top of the other, into his long arms.

He followed Jack up the concrete steps, and Karen, who had seen the van pull up and managed to keep the kids inside until they knew who had come, opened the door for them.

Jack and Mr. Johnson set the boxes down in the middle of the wood floor. The children gathered around, shy but curious. They stared at the unusual stranger's cowboy hat.

"Karen, this is Mr. Johnson," said Jack. "He brought us some Christmas boxes."

Karen looked at the boxes and then at Jack in confusion. Mr. Johnson smiled at her kindly, and his smile seemed to lighten his pale eyes further.

"Thank you," she said, returning his smile and extending her hand. "Our Christmas has been short this year, so we really do appreciate this."

"Oh, it's not from me," Mr. Johnson replied, sweeping the hat from his head to reveal a shock of dark hair. "I'm just delivering it, but I'm glad to see it'll do you folks some good."

"Can I get you anything? Coffee, perhaps?" asked Karen. "And I have sugar cookies if you'd like some."

"They're good," said Nate enthusiastically.

Mr. Johnson smiled at Nate, and then said to Karen, "Thank you, but I have to be going."

He glanced at the large tree and the bare wood floor beneath it, and then he looked at each of the children, barely able to suppress the excitement they felt as they stared at the cardboard boxes and hovered by their mother's side.

"You have beautiful children," he said.

"Thank you," said Jack. "They're good kids."

"I'm sure they are," said Mr. Johnson. "It was a pleasure to meet you all. Enjoy your Christmas."

"Thank you very much," Karen answered.

Then she looked around at her children who had knelt down collectively by the boxes when he mentioned leaving.

Vinca first got the hint.

"Oh, thank you, sir," she said.

"Yes, sir, thank you," said Annie, flipping her blond locks away from her face in preparation to excavate the boxes.

"Merry Christmas, Mr. Johnson," Hoodoo told him, looking up with wonder into his strange, mesmerizing eyes.

Nate got up and stretched out his hand like a gentleman. Mr. Johnson shook it.

"Thank you, sir."

"You're welcome," said Mr. Johnson, his warm gaze taking them all in. "God bless you."

Jack followed him out the door, gripping his hand and shaking it firmly when they reached the van.

"You don't know how much I... my whole family... appreciate this," he said.

Mr. Johnson rested a hand on Jack's shoulder for an instant and smiled. Then he climbed into his vehicle and started the engine. He backed up the van in the dirt by the mailbox and then leaned out the window.

"You know something, Mr. Hoyle," he said, holding Jack's gaze with his own. "Sometimes God doesn't have more important things to do."

He added with a wave, "Merry Christmas!"

Jack was bewildered by these parting words as he watched the van start off down the lane between the barren trees, but suddenly—just before the white vehicle disappeared from sight— his eyes grew wide with comprehension.

Three Boxes

Jack walked slowly across the yard to the front steps. He glanced once more down the lane and entered the house.

Karen came up to him and grabbed his arm. Her brown eyes were huge as she said in a low, constrained voice, "Honey, you have to see this. Everything we asked for is in these boxes."

"What do you mean?" asked Jack.

"Come and see!"

Karen led him by the hand to one of the boxes. She knelt by it and brought out a large ham.

Jack stared at the beautiful pink ham. "Just what you wanted."

"But that's not all," said Karen. She lifted out two long bags of shiny red apples, smiling. "Plenty for your pies."

"And, Vinca," she added excitedly, turning to her daughter, "show your daddy what you found."

Vinca came up to her parents with three rectangular red packages.

"Cordial cherries," she said, offering him one.

"I can't believe it," said Jack, gazing at them with amazement. "What about the other kids?"

Annie, Nate, and Hoodoo looked up from a box full of toys, books, and clothes for children.

"There's art supplies, Dad," said Annie, holding brushes and paint in her hands. "And clothes for us, too. They're nice!"

"I have a G.I. Joe," Nate announced to his dad. He had already opened its box and brought out its vehicle. "It's Frostbite!"

"This is my Barbie," Hoodoo chimed in, a hint of awe in her voice. "She's pretty, isn't she, Daddy?" Still in its big pink box, it was cradled in her arms. Like everything else, it was new. "Do you think God saw our list?" she asked.

Karen turned toward Jack, still bent over the boxes full of Christmas treats and food staples. He was silent for a few moments, gazing down at the boxes, and then he looked up at his wife.

Karen felt the moisture on her face before she was aware that her eyes were full of it. It fell down her cheeks in silent, unsteady streams as Jack gazed at her. The kids were watching their parents. For the moment, neither one could say anything.

When Jack finally spoke, his voice was heavy and unlike itself, filled with wonder. His face, often so intense, was soft and gentle.

"Yes, Hoodoo. I think He must have seen it."

He bent his head once more and pressed his hands into his thighs as he knelt by Karen. She placed her arm around her husband's waist and rested her head on his shoulder.

"Thank God," she whispered.

Vinca joined her parents on the floor by the boxes, embracing her mom and dad, and Hoodoo and Annie quickly followed. Nate looked at his family, congregated in a small, sniffling circle upon the floor, and then, shrugging, he wrapped his sisters in a hug.

Jack lifted his head and attempted to stand up, wiping the back of his hand across his face.

"Well, it looks like we're going to have pie," he said. "And ham!"

"And cordial cherries!" added Vinca, holding them up.

"Yep, we're going to have Christmas dinner, after all."

Karen started to go through the two bags of apples, picking out some for pies.

"Are you going to make pies today, Momma?" Hoodoo asked eagerly.

"Yes, I am."

"Can I help?" asked Annie.

"I'll help, too," said Vinca.

"Let's have some Christmas music," said Jack, going to the radio.

"Will you play some carols on your guitar?" requested Hoodoo, skipping behind her dad.

"Sure. As soon as your mom and sisters are ready."

Joy to the World

Jack did not go back outside to work, for the sun had fallen soon after Mr. Johnson had left the Hoyle home. It was truly Christmas Eve.

As Karen baked in the tiny L-shaped kitchen, it was evident by the quick and easy movement of her hands as she shaped the pastry dough that she enjoyed baking and had a gift for it. One of the few people in the world who, like Bing Crosby, could whistle musically, she whistled favorite Christmas songs as she baked.

She, Vinca, and Annie blended flour, water, and shortening, one of the staples from the food boxes. They got flour all over themselves, a softly descending cloud of Christmas cheer, as they rolled out the dough and placed it in pie plates. Karen sliced the apples, not too small, and mixed them with milk, flour, cinnamon and sugar, and the girls poured them into the pastry. The homemade pie crust was laid carefully over the top, and holes were punctured through with a fork. Two ivory pies were placed in the temperamental oven that Karen guarded to make sure they wouldn't burn.

Jack got out the pipe that his grandfather, an Idaho judge who had died the year Hoodoo was born, had given him. He lit it, throwing the match into the stove, and then he blew smoke rings for his children while the sweet and spicy smell of apple pies baking mingled with them in the air.

The treasured pipe was smoked just once or twice a year on Christmas or New Year's Eve. It was a nostalgic experience for Jack, though his tobacco was old, and the children watched as, on request, he tilted his head back and puffed out large wavering rings of smoke that held a moment as they drifted away and then dissolved.

When the pies were brought out of the oven, they rested on the counter to cool, and the heat struggled away from them, infiltrated the house, and tantalized the nostrils of every member of the household. Each came in a group or alone to admire the pies, and Nate and Hoodoo broke off little pieces of flaky crust again and again as their mom made dinner—until she caught them at it and chased them from her kitchen.

With the ground beef, Karen made her special spaghetti sauce. It was normally a coveted meal for her children, but that night it was merely something to eat quickly, so they could claim a generous slice of apple pie.

The rich, tangy flavor was very persuasive. They devoured a whole pie for dessert, and Nate mourned over the empty plate even though his belly was full.

"Mom, please, please, please make more pies tomorrow."

"We'll see. We have plenty of apples, that's for sure. I do know one thing. We're going to have ham!"

The fire grew lazy and disinterested in producing warmth as the evening wore on. Jack fetched more firewood from outside. Setting it down by the old woodstove, he opened the iron-handled door and shoved a huge log onto the hot coals. Blowing on the fire, drawing his face back after each exhalation, the fire eventually leapt into hot, steady flame.

Jack put another slim log onto it and shut the door firmly. Heat radiated through the room once more, and the dogs and Sammy curled up happily near its source.

Karen, too, stood next to the woodstove, her backside against it to absorb the warmth into her slender frame.

"Are you going to play for us now, honey?" she asked.

"Yeah, are you?" said Hoodoo.

Jack smiled at her.

"Can you say please?"

"Please, Daddy."

"I will if you want."

"Do you want me to get your guitar for you?" Nate asked.

"Sure, son."

Nate went into his parents' bedroom and brought out the hard, black case that held his dad's guitar. The case was worn and plainly told of its travels across the country and of journeying in and out of Nashville's clubs and bars. The cats had used it for a scratching post, too. Nate dragged it with difficulty to his father's feet.

Jack pulled out one of the metal folding chairs from their dining table and sat facing his family. He unsnapped the case and placed the wine-colored Guild on his knee, strumming and tuning it.

"Well," he said. "What do you want to hear?"

"Frosty the Snowman!" cried Hoodoo.

"Come All Ye Faithful," said Karen.

"How about Joy to the World, Daddy?" Vinca asked. "I like the way you play it."

Jack agreed and struck the first chord of "Joy to the World" and began to belt out his rocked-up version of the song in his strong, clear tenor.

Karen and the kids sang with him—Karen in her high angel voice, as Hoodoo called it, and Vinca and Annie in their young sopranos that promised to improve much as they matured. Hoodoo didn't pay any attention to style but, like her dad, belted out the song with gusto, and Nate followed along in a low voice that no one else could hear.

Jack sang "White Christmas" and "Hark! The Herald Angels Sing" and more carols, one after the other. The Christmas tree lights reflected merrily off his shiny red guitar, enhancing the feeling. For a long time, he sang as his children rocked back and forth on the couch to the beat, and Karen softly whistled along with the tune. And, oh! her momma's whistle was at once one of the strangest and loveliest sounds in the world to Hoodoo.

Finally, Jack played "Old Toy Trains" as the night mellowed out and suggested the coming of Christmas morning. Nate stood behind his dad and put an arm around his shoulder as Jack sang the wistful song for his only boy.

Resting her head against Annie's arm and gazing down sleepily at the Barbie in her hands, Hoodoo wondered about the man who had brought her family Christmas. She marveled that Santa was so tall and skinny with a cowboy hat on his head instead of a fur stocking cap. He had not looked at all like how he was pictured in books. But the more she tried to work it out, the less she seemed able to solve the riddle, and her eyes began to droop.

Vinca and Annie sat on either side of their mother. Annie looked down at Hoodoo as her head nodded forward, and then she guided Hoodoo back against the couch, pushing the hair out of her little sister's face. Vinca helped herself to one last cordial cherry before bedtime, as she petted Tommy who lounged on the edge of the couch near her.

Her arms encircling her daughters, Karen felt revived and grateful that the joy and magic of Christmas was something she still experienced though she was no longer a little girl. Looking around at her family in the soft light from the tree and old woodstove, she smiled.

Outside, Jack's singing could be heard along with the steady plucking of his guitar, vaguely and sweetly, as above from the chimney, the wood smoke billowed forth, rising to meet the clouds and wafting off to the east toward the woods, drifting slowly away from the little warm house in Tennessee.

17437263R00080